His green eyes glim...
held hers.

What was it about this man that drew her so? Had the attraction between them always been this intense?

Chuck dipped the spoon back in the ice cream. "This is like when we were dating."

She watched him taste from the silverware he'd just fed her with, unable to take her eyes off him. "I wish I remembered."

"You will," he said confidently.

"And if I don't?"

"Let's work on new memories now." Chuck angled closer, whispering in her ear. "I have an inside track here, knowing what you like."

He pressed his mouth against her neck, just over her leaping pulse. The heat of his breath fanned an answering warmth in her. She lost herself in the sensations he stirred. His mouth grazed up farther to nip her earlobe. He kissed her ear, taking his time.

Finally, his lips moved to hers.

* * *

The Second Chance is part of the Alaskan Oil Barons series from *USA TODAY* bestselling author Catherine Mann!

Dear Reader,

Who remembers the television blockbuster series *Dallas*? Or more recently, *Nashville*? These shows are full of glitz and drama, heartbreak and love, and I adore them and wanted to create that same sweeping family saga feel in my eight-book Alaskan Oil Barons series.

And while it's a blast writing stories with glitz and wealth, I also strive to write characters who are down-to-earth, like those who can be found in the sweeping family sagas of *Friday Night Lights* and *Bloodline*. Alaska offered the perfect setting to give my wealthy characters a grassroots vibe. (And how cool that I get to research by binge watching Netflix!)

Thank you for picking up the next installation of my Alaskan Oil Barons series. I look forward to hearing what you think of Chuck and Shana Mikkelson's story—and updates on the rest of the Steele and Mikkleson families!

Cheers,

CatherineMann.com

CATHERINE MANN

———

THE SECOND CHANCE

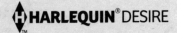

Recycling programs
for this product may
not exist in your area.

ISBN-13: 978-1-335-97185-2

The Second Chance

Printed in U.S.A.

HARLEQUIN®
www.Harlequin.com

USA TODAY bestselling author **Catherine Mann** has won numerous awards for her novels, including both a prestigious RITA® Award and an *RT Book Reviews* Reviewers' Choice Award. After years of moving around the country bringing up four children, Catherine has settled in her home state of South Carolina, where she's active in animal rescue. For more information, visit her website, catherinemann.com.

Books by Catherine Mann

Harlequin Desire

Alaskan Oil Barons

The Baby Claim
The Double Deal
The Love Child
The Twin Birthright
The Second Chance

Visit her Author Profile page at Harlequin.com, or catherinemann.com, for more titles.

To my gifted and delightful editor, Stacy Boyd.

Prologue

Shana had once thought Chuck was the love of her life.

She'd have bet their marriage would last forever.

But today, Shana Mikkelson had to accept that she and Chuck were finished.

Now she just wanted peace, but peace was in short supply as she threw her husband's jeans into a suitcase on their bed. The musky scent of him wafted up from the denim, filling her every breath like a drug she could only quit cold turkey.

Her grief was too deep for tears. Truth be told, there weren't any tears left to shed. She'd just about cried herself into dehydration over this man. She tugged open his dresser drawer, scooped out an armful of socks and strode over to the bed again to dump them into his open luggage.

She kept her eyes on her task and off the bed where they'd made love so often—although not as much lately. She definitely kept her gaze away from her handsome husband, his strong jaw jutting as he threw gear into his shaving kit. Too easily, she could be drawn into the sensual lure of the bristle on his face or the temptation to stroke his perpetually mussed sandy-brown hair. His headful of cowlicks refused to fall in line with the rest of his traditional good looks in a way that somehow made him all the more appealing.

He was like his home state of Alaska, majestic and untamed. Commanding the eye, and yet opaque as a dense forest trailing up a mountainside.

His footsteps sounded along the hardwood floor as he approached her. The storm in his green eyes broadcast his silent protest to her edict that he move out. He was leaving under duress. Well, tough. She'd given him chance after chance. He would cut back at work only to plunge into the office twice as hard again. He wasn't interested in significant change, and over time, that had diluted their love until there was nothing left.

Even their marriage counselor wore a defeated look the last time they'd seen him together.

Every weekly appointment since then? Chuck had canceled. Citing work conflicts—his standard reason for missed dinner dates, too. She'd stopped trusting his word long before that. Trust was already difficult for her, after the way her father had betrayed her and her mother. She didn't think she would ever recover from the blow of finding out her dad had a secret second family.

Chuck's extended absences wore on her. Deeply.

Shana swallowed back the painful past and focused on the present. The heartbreaking present.

They were finally expecting a baby.

After failed fertility treatments and three miscarriages, she'd gotten pregnant by surprise. Very much by surprise as their sex life had been on the rocks along with their marriage.

Their communication was at an all-time low. She needed the controlled setting of their counselor's office to tell her husband about the baby. But since Chuck was a consistent no-show, he still didn't know.

Sitting alone in the counselor's office earlier that day, she'd reached the end of her rope. She was done. She would tell him about the baby once their separation was official. She couldn't afford another emotional breakdown, bad for the health of the baby when Shana was already in such a stressful environment.

She stormed into his closet, wrapped her arms around four of his suits and lifted them from the rack. "This should get you through work until we can set aside a time for you to pick up the rest of your things."

She slammed the bulk of designer suits into his open case on the bed.

"Shana, I'm sorry for missing the appointment." He paced barefoot, faded jeans hugging his muscular thighs, his long-sleeved tee stretching across his broad shoulders. His hair was still damp from the shower he'd taken after work. "You have to understand the business merger comes with extra hours. I've bowed out of as many things as I can."

Since the Mikkelson matriarch had married the Steele patriarch, the two former rival oil families were merging their families' companies into Alaska Oil Barons, Inc. The lengthy process had siblings from both sides making power grabs at a time when stockholders needed to see unity.

"And yet you're still secluded in the study every night."

They did nothing together except sleep and eat. No more days spent horseback riding, snowmobiling and traveling. And as much as she wanted to trust Chuck that it was only work and that things would change, she could only bury her head in the sand for so long before she smothered to death.

"I'm doing my best, Shana. Things will get better as the merger takes root."

"So you keep saying." She tossed a handful of silk ties into the suitcase. "Every deadline you give for this magical easing at work just gets pushed back. I feel like a fool for believing you."

"Damn it, Shana, you've got to see the effort." He

forked his hand through his hair. "I even had my antisocial brother stand in for me at that wildlife preservation fund-raiser. There aren't as many Mikkelsons as there are Steeles. And with Mom and Glenna both married to Steeles, their loyalties are split in a way mine aren't. I'm a Mikkelson. Period."

As was the baby he knew nothing about.

Thinking about raising their child alone made her heart and head ache. Chuck would want to be a part of the child's life. She didn't doubt that. She just wasn't sure how much time he would make for the baby.

Her ability to trust him had been eroded on so many levels.

Resolve strengthened, she faced him. "It's quite clear where your heart lies."

"That's not fair, Shana. These are extreme times. If I scale back too much, the Steele family could eclipse our vision and our power," he said, sitting on the edge of the bed. Their bed. Nearly four years ago, when they'd married and built their dream home in Anchorage, she'd decorated their bedroom with such romantic hope in each detail of the modern French provincial decor.

They'd spent a lot of hours in this room—making love, sharing dreams. Until the third miscarriage had taken too much of a toll on both of them.

"Then by all means, don't let me hold you back. *Dig in*." She closed his suitcase with a decisive click and spun away hard and fast.

Too fast. The room spun and she gripped the footboard of the bed to keep from stumbling.

"Shana?"

She blinked fast to clear the spots dancing in front of her eyes, to quell the nausea from her blossoming headache.

If she could just get Chuck to leave so she could lie down and breathe…

"Please. Go." She pushed free the two words, a mammoth undertaking with her stress headache spiking.

Why was he walking so slowly? She saw his mouth moving, but nothing was coming out. That didn't make sense. And then he tipped.

Except no.

The whole room tipped because…

Her hand slid from the bed on her way to the floor.

One

Thirty-six hours later

Until today, Charles "Chuck" Mikkelson had run out of ideas for a second chance with his wife. Admitting defeat had never been an option for him, professionally or personally.

But amnesia as a do-over with Shana was extreme, even for him.

Surely he'd heard the neurologist wrong. Chuck's gut knotted. "Do you mean Shana is disoriented? Fuzzy on things like the time or date? Forgot what she had for dinner?"

After all, she'd suffered a minor aneurysm that had left her unconscious for just over thirty-six hours. The longest day and a half of his life. But finally, she was awake. Alive.

Two physicians occupied the secluded sitting area where Chuck had been brought after a staffer located him grabbing a bite in the cafeteria while a privately hired nurse sat with Shana. Chuck couldn't believe his wife had actually woken up the one time he'd stepped away from her hospital room. The neurologist—Dr. Harris—sat beside Chuck. Another of Shana's physicians stood at the window. Snow was coming down in thick sheets of white, as if the hospital sterility was outside as well as indoors.

"Shana *is* disoriented, but it's more than that," Dr. Harris explained slowly from the chrome-and-leather chair he'd pulled around to face Chuck. "You need to accept that she has lost her memory."

Amnesia. The word still ricocheted around in Chuck's brain. "She doesn't know who she is?"

Dr. Harris closed the tablet that he'd used earlier to show the part of her brain that was affected. "Actually, she does know her name. She recalls details about herself. The memory loss focuses on more recent events."

"How recent?" Chuck asked, unease creeping up his spine.

"She has the month correct. But five years prior."

Five years ago? That meant… "She doesn't remember anything about me."

Much less about being married to him. There were some times between them lately he wouldn't mind forgetting. But the thought of losing memories of the good times with Shana?

Unthinkable.

The two doctors exchanged somber looks before Shana's other doctor took a seat in the other wing-back. Dr. Gibson was young, but tops when it came to fertility specialists. It meant a lot to Chuck that the man had shown up to weigh in on Shana's condition even though they weren't trying for another baby.

"Chuck, I'm sorry to say, she does not remember you," Dr. Gibson said in the quietly comforting tone he'd used during Chuck and Shana's failed in vitro and three miscarriages. A phantom sucker punch to the gut wracked Chuck.

It had been bittersweet when Dr. Gibson had assisted in caring for Chuck's stepsister two months ago, after she delivered twins in a car. Pretending nothing was wrong had been hard as hell for Chuck, and Shana hadn't wanted his comfort.

"We were having trouble. Do you think this memory loss is more psychological than physical?"

He'd blamed himself repeatedly for this aneurysm. If they hadn't been fighting, if intense emotions hadn't raised her blood pressure, maybe this wouldn't have happened.

"There's no question she's had an aneurysm, and she's incredibly lucky to have come through it so well. But that's not to say there aren't psychological aspects in play. The body and mind work in tandem."

Staring at the tablet in the doctor's hand, Chuck

moved toward a planter, something to rest on. "How do we proceed from here? What do we tell her, and what's her prognosis?"

"I realize that you need answers, but it's too early to project the long term. For now, the counselor on staff here suggests we answer questions as she asks them, no additional information," Dr. Harris warned. "A psychiatrist will be consulting. Things are still so very new."

The obstetrician leaned forward, elbows on his knees. "Let's focus on the positives. Shana's awake and physically fine. The baby's heartbeat is strong. That's news to celebrate."

Chuck frowned, certain he'd misunderstood. Gibson had to be confusing patients after a late shift.

Dr. Harris straightened. "The baby?"

"What baby?" Chuck said precisely. Because no way could Shana be pregnant now of all times. The dark irony of that would be too much to entertain.

Dr. Gibson's eyebrows shot up before he schooled his face back into an alarmingly blank expression. "She didn't tell you about the pregnancy?"

Chuck shook his head slowly, stunned, half-certain there was an error. Fate couldn't be this twisted.

"Shana is expecting," he said baldly. "Two months along. And from your reaction, Chuck, she hadn't told you yet."

Chuck sifted through the hell of the past day and a half. There hadn't been any need to call Dr. Gibson in on the case on a weekend. Chuck had said no to the possibility of pregnancy when the admission staff had asked.

Now he realized the truth of it. Shana had gotten pregnant without an in vitro procedure.

The reality slammed into Chuck like a ton of bricks. Against all odds, they were expecting a child.

Now.

He couldn't even sort through the layers of "stunned" to feel anything but shock.

Chuck's mind winged back to their attending the baptism for his sister Glenna's daughter. He and Shana had actually spent a week getting along, drawn into their hopes for the future, loving their niece and considering adoption. Glenna clearly loved Fleur, no biological bond needed.

Emotions running high, Chuck and Shana had spent a week in bed together. A week that had apparently defied their odds and borne fruit. He had to be there for Shana and their child.

Dr. Harris opened his tablet again, scrolling through his notes. "While I wish we had known so we could have monitored the fetus, none of the medications she's received should present a risk to the baby's development. We'll keep Shana another night for monitoring."

Dr. Gibson said, "We'll also do an ultrasound and start her on progesterone given her prior miscarriages."

Chuck nodded, still reeling. A baby. She was two months along. She'd known and she hadn't told him.

Worse yet, she'd thrown him out without telling him she carried his child.

She'd probably realized that if she told him about the baby, it would have taken a force of nature to budge him from their house. He didn't have the luxury of anger right now.

Dr. Gibson tilted his head, placing a hand on Chuck's shoulder. "I realize this is difficult for you, too. You've both been waiting for this baby for so long, and these aren't the circumstances anyone could have foreseen." He gestured toward the door. "Perhaps seeing you will jog her memory."

And therein lay his problem.

He didn't want her to remember.

Because if she did?

Shana would walk, taking their baby with her.

Shana pushed herself up on the hospital bed, taking her time to be sure the room didn't spin as it had the last time she'd tried. People were acting strange around her, and she wanted answers. Instead, she was stuck lying here alone with only a view of snow slamming down on the mountains.

Well, alone except for a nurse who'd been there since she'd woken up and hadn't left her side, even when the doctors stopped by, doctors who'd been short of answers as to why she was here. Even her phone was missing and the remote control for the TV wasn't working. The nurse said it would be fixed soon.

Shana touched her head, exploring her hairline. A small bandage was located just behind her ear. She'd been assured her long hair covered the shaved patch. The doctor had only told her she'd suffered a minor aneurysm, but that otherwise she was physically fine. Beyond that, they'd been cagey.

Thinking back, she tried to remember what had happened before she'd come to the hospital. The last thing she recalled was an argument with her mother over Shana's refusal to reconcile with her father. Even thinking about the fight and her dad made her headache worse.

She knew avoidance when she heard it. Her work as a private detective had taught her all the signs. She also had a sixth sense for these things and trusted her gut.

Something was going on beyond what they'd told her.

Turning to the nurse, who was making updates on the dry-erase board in her room, Shana asked, "Excuse me? When will the doctor be back? I have questions."

Being in limbo was scary. Her imagination was working overtime.

Just as the nurse opened her mouth to answer, a knock sounded and the door opened to admit a man. Not the doctor who'd been by to check her out when she'd woken. And even though it felt like a slew of staff had come through her room in the past half hour, she would have remembered this guy. He had an unforgettable face, movie-star quality in a rough-around-the-edges way. His light brown hair was just long enough to be mussed by a woman's fingers, coarse hair that would rasp the skin.

A doctor? He didn't have on a white coat. In fact, he was dressed more casually than any doctor she knew. He wore jeans and a long-sleeved T-shirt that bore the wrinkles of someone who'd pulled a long shift. But his sea green eyes were what held her attention in an unbreakable grip. The colors shifted with the icy intensity of a winter sea.

What crazy thoughts to be having right now, but the tug of attraction made her feel normal on a day that was entirely too abnormal.

"I appreciate that you're all being thorough, but I need to get in touch with my mother. I just want to call her, and no one will give me a phone."

Or a remote control. Or a mirror. Or answers.

Okay, this was getting really weird.

Strangely, the nurse left the room. Physicians usually kept a nurse with them for exams. Although the door had been left open.

"Your mother is on her way. She should be here tomorrow." He stopped by the bed, large hands grasping the bedrail.

Before she could help herself, she checked his ring finger and found...

A wedding band.

Disappointment cooled the attraction. So much for drooling over Mr. Cover Model. She pressed her fingers to her forehead. She should be focused on more serious matters rather than this sexy distraction.

"Which doctor are you?" She settled on the reasonable question, a thousand more zipping around in her fuzzy brain.

"You should rest," he said evasively. "You've been through a lot. Your body needs to recharge."

"Aren't you a doctor?" She massaged her temple. "Or an occupational therapist? I can't recall. There were so many people in the room when I woke up."

"I'm not your doctor."

A nervous skitter started up her spine, like something shifting behind a mist, just out of reach. "Remind me who you are?"

"My name is Chuck, and I'm going to get your doctor." He backed up a step. "Things are…complicated."

"Well, Chuck, I've had people checking me and asking questions, but no one has been answering mine." Panic rose inside her. "Tell me what's going on, or give me a phone to speak to my mother. Why are you keeping her from me?"

"Your mother is flying in." He held up a calming, reassuring hand that somehow only made things worse. "She's not available to talk yet."

A pit formed deep in her belly. The walls bore down on her.

Nothing was as it seemed.

This place was starting to feel like a jail, except the private room full of high-tech equipment and flowers was far too posh for incarceration. She needed to get her life in order, call her mom, check in with her boss about her caseload and an upcoming court case she would be testifying in.

"Then I guess that leaves you or the doctor to tell me, because lying here waiting is most definitely stressing me out." She swung her legs out from under the sheet.

The room spun.

Chuck rushed forward and clasped her arm. His touch was at once both steadying and unsettling.

Her gaze went back to that glinting wedding band. The spark of awareness made her feel ill. Married cheaters were the worst. Her father's deceit had left a wake of devastation. The room started spinning again but in a different way from having wobbly legs.

Something was wrong here. Very wrong.

"I need to know what's going on and if you won't tell me—" she reached for the call button "—then I'm going to find someone who will."

He released her arm. "Okay, we'll talk. There's no agenda here other than looking out for your health. Any question you have, I will answer honestly."

Alarms went off in her mind. When people said words like *honestly* and *truthfully*, that usually meant they had something to lie about. "I want to know why everyone is acting so strange around me."

"The aneurysm has affected your memory," he said slowly, carefully.

Her *memory*? The weight of that word hit her hard. "How so?"

"You've forgotten the past five years."

His words slammed into her, adding a push to that merry-go-round feel in her head. "Five years? Gone. And we know each other?"

Even as her world spiraled, the confusion faded as the logical answer came together—his lack of a medical coat, his familiarity...and the wedding band.

Face somber, Chuck rested his hands on her shoulders, holding her gaze with his. "We more than know each other. I'm your husband."

The horrified expression on Shana's face was damn near insulting. Her gaze shot to his wedding band, then back up to his eyes.

Color drained from her already pale face. She sagged back down into the hospital bed, her blond hair splashing across the pillow. He wanted to protect her, to find some way to wrestle their problems into submission. Not that he'd ever had much luck with that. He needed to put aside his own feelings and focus on her. Focus on keeping her calm—and making the most of this time to heal the rift between them.

Shana thumbed her own bare ring finger. "Married? To each other?"

"For almost four years. Your jewelry was taken off when you were admitted to the hospital." He tapped her ring finger lightly, the softness of her skin so familiar—and seductive. Even in the middle of the worst crisis of his life.

She had a beauty and fire that rocked even a hospital gown.

"You're my husband? I… Why… What happened? This is, um, overwhelming."

"I realize it's a lot to absorb." He pulled a chair closer and sat, taking both of her hands in his. "The doctor said the memory loss could be temporary."

"Or it could be permanent." She didn't pull away, but she did look at their clasped hands with confusion. "How long have we known each other?"

Those soft blue eyes turned hawkish, reading him like an X-ray machine. He nodded, clearing his throat. Determined to deliver objective facts. To not make this worse.

"We met nearly five years ago." He watched her closely to gauge her reaction. He felt like he knew her so well, but also not at all.

How much of the essence of Shana would still exist with the memory loss?

Questions flooded his mind with too many potential futures to absorb at once.

"So my amnesia starts from right before I met you?" she said slowly, suspicion filling her eyes.

She was too astute. It seemed her private investigator skills were as honed as ever.

"It appears so," he said, treading carefully through this discussion that was full of land mines. "I don't expect you to take my word for anything. Talk to my family, talk to your mother, whatever you need to do to feel reassured."

"You have family nearby?"

"I do. A large family. My mother and some of my siblings live in Anchorage, except for my brother, who's closer to Juneau." He shared the details carefully, watching for signs of recollection. Her amnesia could disappear at any moment and she would go back to tossing him out on his ass. "My mother recently remarried and her new husband has an even larger family, mostly local, too."

"A big family is a blessing." Her blue eyes shone with a pain he recognized.

Learning of her father's hidden second family had wounded Shana deeply as a teen. She had three half siblings she'd never met. Her father's betrayal had cut so deeply that Shana still had trouble trusting. Chuck knew he needed to keep that in mind now more than ever. If he made a misstep, this could go so very wrong.

But he couldn't let her go, especially not now.

He would do what was necessary to protect Shana, and their unborn baby.

There'd been a time when they talked of having at least four children. Life had a different plan for them.

"Considering my family and Mom's new husband's family have been business enemies for decades, we weren't sure about the blessing part at first. Family reunions are dicey, but it's starting to shake out."

"So you and I are happily married?"

Now, there was a loaded question. "We had our problems like any other couple," he hedged.

The last thing he wanted to lead with was their hellish fight right before her aneurysm, a fight that had her hauling his clothes from the closet as she told him to move out. But the doctor had said to answer honestly. He could offer up part of their issues without tipping his hand. "We had been going through fertility treatments to start a family, and that put a strain on us."

"But we were committed enough that we wanted a child together."

"*Want* a child. Present tense." He very much intended to be a full-time father to their child. If this pregnancy went well, Chuck would do everything in his power to be there for his kid.

"You have to realize I'm overwhelmed by all of this." She threaded her fingers through her long, honeyed hair, over her ear, her eyes widening. "Amnesia? It's something we all know about, but I never imagined it could actually happen to me."

"Of course. It's a lot. Take your time. I'm here for you, whatever you need, and I'm not going anywhere."

"Thank you—" She frowned, pressing her temples.

"People call me Chuck," he reminded her. "Or Charles."

"What did I call you?"

The last time they'd been together, she'd called

him a list of names better left unsaid right now. "You called me Chuck."

"Thank you, Chuck."

The way her voice wrapped around his name sounded as familiar as ever.

A tap sounded on the door. "Hello?"

A recognizable voice called out an instant before the door opened to the youngest of his siblings— Alayna.

The shiest of them all, she entered hesitantly. There'd been a time as a child when she was as talkative as the rest of them, but then she'd changed. Withdrawn. Telling her to leave would be like plucking wings off a butterfly.

But he'd hoped to keep his family out of this situation a little while longer until he could explain the amnesia to them. Alayna had a quiet way of slipping past people's defenses. While the family probably hadn't noticed she'd left, the staff here likely had been charmed and unaware she was supposed to be anywhere but here.

Hell, even he couldn't find it in himself to be mad at her for caring so much.

Alayna rushed to Shana's bedside and hugged her gently. "Thank goodness you're awake. I've been so worried."

Shana stared over his sister's shoulder with wide, surprised eyes. "Uh, hello, thank you."

Stepping back, Alayna sank into a chair. "I'm so

relieved you're awake, and healthy, and the baby's okay. It's a miracle."

How the hell had she heard the news? And damn, he needed to say something quickly before—

Shana's surprised look shifted to outright stunned.

"The baby?"

Two

A baby?

Panic and confusion rocked Shana, the young woman's voice still ringing in her ears. She had a child as well as a husband? Her hand slid to her stomach, still flat. Surely there must be some kind of mistake.

Unless they meant a child that had already been born.

"We have a child?" Shana asked, her mind spinning. "How old? You say the child's okay. Did something happen when I had the aneurysm? Was I driving a car or holding—?"

"Nothing like that." He looked sideways at

Alayna, who appeared even more confused than Shana felt.

Slack-jawed, the young woman—late teens, perhaps?—glanced back and forth between them. "I don't understand—"

Chuck placed a silencing hand on the girl's shoulder. "Shana, I'd hoped to share this more carefully, but here goes. You're eight weeks pregnant."

Air whooshed from her lungs. Her ears rang. She could barely wrap her brain around this latest shock. "It's… I…um, I don't know what to say."

The young woman tugged on her overlong sweater nervously, tears welling in her eyes. "I'm sorry. I didn't mean to… Well, I'm just so sorry."

Chuck slung an arm around her shoulders and gave her a comforting squeeze even though his eyes broadcast frustration. "Meet my sister." He turned to the younger woman. "Alayna, Shana's suffering from temporary amnesia and has forgotten about the past five years. You couldn't have known. Although I'm curious as hell how you heard about the pregnancy."

Alayna chewed her already short fingernails. "I thought… Oh my. I'm sorry. I was walking by the nurses' station and overheard them talking about things for shift change… I'm really sorry."

Chuck pulled a tight smile. "It's going to be okay, kiddo. Shana just has some gaps in her memory. It'll all sort out."

Shana wished she could be as confident about that. She'd thought about being a mom someday, but this was too much too fast. Not that it seemed she had any choice in the matter. Her life was on warp speed.

Her father had wrecked her mother's life. Shana had always known when it was her time to be a parent, the decision would have to be made slowly and carefully. If she and Chuck had been trying for a child, then their marriage must have been solid.

So why didn't she feel like the love-at-first-sight lightning bolt had hit her? Lust maybe, but not love.

"Shana, I'm really sorry to have confused you or made things more difficult." Fidgeting, Alayna ducked out from under her brother's arm and stood. "I'll just leave, and we can talk another time when things are less, well, confusing. I'm so sorry."

"It's okay."

Or rather, she hoped it would be. Shana exhaled hard, unsure how she felt about carrying a child she couldn't recall conceiving versus there being a child already in the picture, a child she also wouldn't have remembered giving birth to.

Alayna held up a hand. "I really do apologize." She backed away. "I love you to pieces, Shana."

Standing, Chuck cupped Alayna's shoulder. "If you could get coffee for me I would appreciate it." He pulled a twenty out of his wallet. "Get something for yourself, too. Thanks, kiddo."

Once the door closed, Shana pushed herself up to sit straighter in the bed, unsure when she'd sunk into a slouch.

Chuck rubbed the back of his neck, frustration

in his eyes. "I apologize for not managing the news better."

"How could you have predicted any of this? No one could." An understatement.

"You're being too understanding." He sank back in the chair by her bed.

"Well, I do have some questions." Even thinking about the possibilities sent a fresh wave of panic through her, but not knowing was worse. "The child is yours, right?"

"Absolutely yes," he said without hesitation. "The baby is mine. And no, we don't have any other children."

She hadn't even considered that. But what else didn't she know? Five years was a long time to make significant memories. Life-changing memories.

"You said we'd struggled with fertility." She chewed her fingernail. "There's just so much to learn about what's happened over the past five years."

And her brain was on overload, weighing every nugget of information before she trusted the latest revelation. Even well-meaning people had private agendas. And she also knew how easily a person could be misled by someone smooth at lying. Her father had taught her that lesson too painfully.

"Then we won't press any further today." He covered her hand with his and held tight. "I would really feel more comfortable if we called the doctors back in and let them check you over or give us more guidance."

His touch felt…familiar somehow. Strong, yet careful all at once.

She couldn't deny the wisdom in his words. "I just want to know one more thing for now."

He grinned—the first time she'd seen him smile, or remembered seeing him smile—and it shone from his eyes, setting her senses buzzing.

He was sheer magnetism personified.

"Like I have the option of arguing with you?"

She couldn't help but smile back. "Apparently you do know me well. Better than I know myself at the moment, which brings me to my question. What's my last name? Or rather, what's your last name? Did I keep my maiden name?"

His smile faded and he clasped her hand, the left one without a wedding ring. "You took my surname. It's Mikkelson."

Surprise spread through her. "As in the oil family Mikkelsons?"

"Yes, the same." He nodded.

There was a wariness to him she couldn't quite understand. Maybe people befriended him for his money. That would have never crossed her mind. Still, a lot of things made more sense now.

"No wonder I have this private room. Your parents own Mikkelson Oil." She pressed her fingers to the headache starting again.

"It's not Mikkelson Oil anymore. My father passed away nearly three years ago. My mother recently married the head of Steele Oil—widower Jack

Steele—merging the two companies into Alaska Oil Barons, Inc."

For what should be big news, he didn't look all that happy about it.

"I'm sorry about your father." She squeezed his hand and a shiver of electricity passed between them, like static popping through her.

His thumb stroked along the inside of her wrist over her speeding pulse. "Thank you. He was fond of you."

"I wish I remembered that."

"Me too."

Awareness increased until the static between them was like a meteor shower. Beautiful...but something she feared could leave her scorched.

The door opened again with a call at the same time. "Dr. Gibson here."

Chuck cleared his throat and stepped back. "He's your ob-gyn."

Dr. Gibson entered, wheeling a machine of some sort, with a nurse trailing behind. "I hear the two of you were going to have a discussion."

Chuck nodded. "I've told Shana I'm her husband, and she knows about the baby."

"How are you feeling?" Dr. Gibson stopped beside her bed.

"Overwhelmed. A little woozy. But mostly just confused."

"That's understandable," he said with a kind bedside manner that must have been reassuring during all the fertility treatments Chuck had mentioned. "The nurse is going to check your blood pressure, and then we're going to do an ultrasound. We'll go as slowly as you need us to."

Shana's heart skipped a beat. So much was happening so quickly she wanted to tell them all to slow down, to stop altogether. But life didn't work that way. She had to face the present. "No need to wait. I want to know as much as I can."

"Ask anything you like, and I'll do my best to answer," Dr. Gibson said. "Are you all right with Mr. Mikkelson staying in the room? I understand these are rather unusual circumstances."

Shana looked at Chuck. He was her husband. Everyone here knew that. And this was his child. As strange as it felt to have him in the room, he had a right to be here. The past day must have been hellish for him with her health scare. "Of course he can stay."

"Thank you." Chuck took her hand in his, his touch strong and confident.

Those green eyes of his held her, reminding her again of a changeable rolling sea. She could so easily dive in, immerse herself in him.

Lose herself.

And that made him dangerous.

Her first priority right now was deciphering who she was.

She couldn't afford to let down her guard around the one man she should be able to trust with her life.

* * *

The next day, as Chuck checked Shana out of the hospital, he was still reeling from seeing that ultrasound.

Snow gathered on the ground. The blacktop parking lot looked more like a field than a place for cars. But he, too, felt like he'd fallen away from the present moment.

He recalled instead a different moment. The first time Shana had announced a pregnancy. The promise and hope of that moment. So different than this one.

He had fantasized about a future with Shana and a kid on the way, but in no realm had his fantasies played out this way. They'd watched ultrasounds together in the past, but they had given up on ever seeing one again.

And now, Chuck was preparing to take his pregnant wife home.

A wife who didn't remember him.

He stepped out of the hospital and into the crisp morning air, an orderly wheeling Shana beside Chuck. His personal staffer had brought around his Escalade, the exhaust puffing clouds into the cold. The snow was pristine after yesterday's storm, piles on the side of the roads from snowplows clearing the way.

As the driver opened the passenger door and left the engine running for Chuck to drive, Chuck held out his hand for his wife. His pregnant wife.

The ultrasound had made this so real.

There was a baby in the mix of this insane time in his life—the merger, the long hours, the amnesia, and a second chance with Shana he didn't want to waste.

Growing up, he'd dreamed of having a perfect marriage like his parents. That wasn't going to happen. He and Shana had too much water under the bridge, and for too long.

But Chuck had never failed at anything in his life. He didn't want his marriage to be the first. Which meant he needed to use this time together to win over his wife.

Shana spent much of the drive back home in a state of shock, mixed with wary hope that surely her memory would be jogged by something. Soon.

So far, no luck.

The streets leading away from the hospital had markers of familiarity, but her mind whirred. Her memory of the main highway was five years out of date.

Five years.

Such a significant amount of time. She tried to conjure up a holiday, an image of her wedding day. Tried to imagine where she might have tied the knot. Wondered who her best friend was.

But no memories pounded against her mind's eye. Just an ultrasound image and a cyclone of questions.

Questions that hammered harder at her chest as they pulled up to their house. Her home. The home she shared with Chuck, heir to an oil empire and sexy as hell in a Stetson. Chuck had told her that her mother would be going straight from the airport to their house. There had been some delays with her flight.

And as they turned the corner, Shana took in the mammoth structure, eyes moving past the snow-covered arbor to the chimney puffing gray smoke rings against the iced sky. So many rooms, so many memories that refused to materialize. Had they picked this place out together? Had she determined which trees should be placed where?

The automatic security gate slid back to reveal a clear view of the massive two-story house with a French country charm. More of that wary hope filled her as she studied the home and grounds. Would she recognize any of it? Whitewashed brick and porches. So many porches on every floor, enclosed and open, as if there was enough space to accommodate any season.

Beautiful, but unfamiliar.

She'd grown up with security, in a cute ranch-style home made of brick. Her mother had worked at the local air force base as a nurse. Her father had always claimed he was short of money. She'd heard her parents fight about it. Sometimes the words were distinguishable, most of the time not. But in the words that had trickled through, her mom had accused him of having a drinking problem. Another time she'd questioned him about a gambling addiction, even other women. The possibility of him supporting a whole second family had never come up, so far as Shana had known.

Who would suspect that?

God, trust was tough, but right now she wasn't in a position to walk away. She didn't even know who she was.

And if this pregnancy lasted, she wanted to give her child a chance at a loving home and family.

She shook off the past. She hated dwelling on such negative notions and letting her father have real estate in her brain. He didn't deserve so much as a passing thought. Instead, she focused on the house where, according to Chuck, she'd lived for nearly four years.

The property seemed to be about five acres. In addition to the mansion, the grounds had a small barn and a five-car garage. High-end cars lined the driveway, snow billowing down on them. The counselor had encouraged her to have a controlled meeting of the family as early as Shana could agree to it. Shana had replied that the tension of wondering was worse.

So Chuck's family was here, waiting for her arrival.

If only the curtain would rise, revealing her past. This was a magnificent place set against the mountain range. Would she feel more at peace when she saw the decor? Would she recognize her influence in the home?

Modern French provincial was her style. A promising omen.

"Did we decorate together, or did you leave it all to me?"

"We chose artwork together, but the rest is all you." His face was angular in the glow from the dash. With the sun setting early, the headlights cast stripes ahead as he neared their home, passing a frozen pond.

"Were you okay with that?"

"Completely. We blended both of our tastes where it mattered to me. For example, I had some antlers from a hunting trip with my father that I wanted to keep, and you honored that wish in a thoughtful way."

"How so?"

He parked under a portico, the vehicle still running, heat pumping. "You incorporated them into a massive chandelier with candles over our dining room table. It's a great tribute to my dad."

The nostalgia in his voice drew her closer.

"I wish I could remember having met him." Or remember any of the past five years with Chuck. She swallowed, frustrated at the void. The not knowing.

Chuck stroked her hair back from her face. "Losing him was hard on all of us. For you, too."

Her hand gravitated to his jaw and she let herself test the bristly feel of him under the guise of offering comfort. "You're named for him."

"You remember?" He looked up sharply, those attentive eyes causing her cheeks to heat.

"Not the way you mean. It's more of a guess that

feels right." She couldn't miss the wariness in his eyes, something that hinted he would rather she didn't remember. A shiver rippled through her and she pulled her hand away. "Although I don't have a clue who each of those cars belongs to."

He pointed to the first car. "That's my mother's. She wanted to see you in the hospital, but I didn't want you overwhelmed with new faces."

Was that true? Or did his family not like her and that's why only his younger sister had been around?

Either way, he'd been right to keep them away from the hospital, because with Shana's memory of the past five years still a no-show, she was starting to panic over going into her house emotionally blind to re-meet so many people who already knew her.

Maybe having them come over hadn't been such a great idea after all.

But now it was too late to go back.

As the thick door swung open and she stepped through, a sheer mass of humanity greeted her. When Chuck said he had a big family, she hadn't fully comprehended what that meant.

Her eyes flicked as she tried to take in all these new—and yet not new—people and this house at the same time. A tall blonde woman with a baby on her hip leaned against the iron railing of the staircase, her smile warm and welcoming. A cluster of people stood on the white-and-brown-dappled fur rug, crowding around the plush chairs.

Chuck pronounced their names as they moved,

but Shana's head throbbed at all the information. She tried to imagine picking out the furniture with the man who held her steady as she pushed through a barrage of people.

People who seemed genuinely concerned for her. People who felt like strangers.

They moved further into the house, her hand reaching out to touch the wall as they turned from the entry hall into the dining room. Her eyes scanned the long wooden table flanked by eight large chairs. It held a table setting for two.

A snapshot of daily life.

Bouquets of fresh flowers and tall candles ran down the table's spine. A familiar touch—a tradition from her mother. She'd brought that here, to her life as a married woman.

A small comfort. But a comfort she embraced, the kind of nod from the universe that something made sense. It gave her the strength to meet even more people.

It helped to divide them into two family trees rather than take them in as one mass of blended family. Chuck's mother, Jeannie, was head of the Mikkelson clan with two sons and two daughters. Jack Steele—Jeannie's new husband—had five adult children, three sons and two daughters. His oldest son was married to Chuck's oldest sister, and the couple had a baby girl. The oldest Steele daughter was married to a scientist and they had twin baby girls.

Shana's heart tugged at the sight of those little ones, reminding her of the child she'd only just learned she carried but that she already loved. Somewhere in the back of her mind, she recalled hearing that Jack had lost his wife and another daughter in a plane crash over fifteen years ago. It had probably been big news across the state at the time, given the prominence of this family.

"It's kind of you all to come greet me." She sank into one of the chairs in the living room, Chuck staying close behind her. His presence, the touch of his hand to her shoulder, stirred something in her. A feeling. A pull. A recognition.

But the touch couldn't assuage her frustration or the dizzying impact of re-meeting five years' worth of connections. She glanced up at Chuck, his sandy-brown hair tousled upward. It caught the light reflecting off the mirror that hung above the mantel.

A mirror world indeed.

She struggled to force that memory of ordering the piece to her mind's eye. Even as she studied the antlers in front of her, she failed to locate the story from her perspective. All that Shana had was the retelling of a memory that Chuck had shared with her.

As if he knew her distress, Chuck gave her shoulder a quick squeeze.

The smile lines on Jeannie's face deepened. A warm smile. One Shana wanted to take comfort in. The older woman gave a knowing nod. "I can tell by Chuck's face that he thinks we're overwhelming you. But when we heard your mother's flight was delayed for snow, we wanted to bring you something to welcome you home. We're here just to lay eyes on you, bring you food, then be on our way."

"You're hoping that if I see you, it'll jog my memory. I'm sorry, but it doesn't. I may never remember. Thank you for trying, though. For caring." She swallowed, hard. Leaned back into the wooden chair. Looked at the faces of the Mikkelsons and the Steeles. Noted how comfortable they seemed around the long dining room table. Knew their appearance here to be motivated by love.

Somehow that recognition pained her.

"I'm just glad you're alive and well," Jeannie said. "And know we're all only a phone call away if you have any questions."

"I appreciate it. Please stay for dinner." Shana bit her lip. Wishing she had something more to say. Wishing this whole meeting could somehow miraculously deliver up the memories she sought, for herself and for her child. And for this sexy man at her side? For the love she must have lost?

Why was it so difficult to wrap her brain around?

Disappointment swamped her.

In spite of Chuck's family's warm welcome, Shana still couldn't shake an unsettled feeling.

She couldn't stop searching for a reason why she was so certain there was trouble in paradise.

Three

Chuck leaned on the door frame, hand up in a static wave as darkness flooded the horizon. The light from his sister's car blinded him ever so briefly as she threw her SUV into Reverse. He was still unsure how the events of the last several hours had gone.

Running a hand through his thick hair, he stretched, his neck popping. Releasing some of the tension he'd carried.

The night had been an exercise in dodging one land mine after another, worrying about what his family might reveal. He appreciated their concern, and Shana had been emphatic about seeing them, hoping somehow that their appearance would break the dam to release her memories.

All the more reason for him to hustle them out the door. If only he'd managed to dissuade Shana from inviting them in the first place. But to push her to wait would have made her suspicious. He needed her calm. He needed to gain time with Shana, time enough to forge a connection strong enough that she wouldn't leave.

All the more reason he was glad to see his family off. Finally, the last of them had left. Exhaling hard, Chuck closed the door and armed the security system.

Shana should be resting. She was fresh out of the hospital, pregnant and disoriented. Although she'd seemed to welcome the distraction of other people in the house, most likely to keep from being alone with him.

At least his family had been sensitive enough not to mention their marital problems. However, his mother had pulled out photo albums in an attempt to help jog Shana's memories—including his and Shana's wedding pictures, none of which had sparked the least bit of remembrance. A relief. And strangely irksome as well.

Chuck scrubbed a hand over his jaw, striding past the dining room, cleared by extra staff he'd hired to help during Shana's recovery. Even though he now employed a chef, his family had left behind enough food for an army even though they'd all eaten their fill until the candles had burned down in the silver candelabras. Even as he'd wished them gone, he'd been grateful for the positive spin they'd put on his marriage. Their presence had given off a happy family vibe he needed to stress with his wife.

As much as he told himself to take one day at a time, Chuck found he needed to have this settled, to know Shana would be staying with him. There was no room for compromise on this matter.

A few steps farther down the corridor, he discovered Shana in the study, reading on the sofa, a mug of hot cocoa on the coffee table. A blaze roared in the fireplace. Above, snow piled on the skylights, hiding nearly all of the inky night sky. Her hair was loose down her back, her legs curled up under her.

So many times, he'd found her like this in the past. In the early days of their marriage, he wouldn't have thought twice about joining her there, skimming his hands up her lovely legs. Kissing her senseless. Peeling her clothes away until they were both naked, the firelight licking shadows over their skin.

At one time, he'd thought they had a future. Now...

He had to ensure that her future—his child's future—included him.

Perhaps he could recover some ease with her in this room, in a space where they'd been happy. So often they'd shared time in the study, both of them in here while he'd worked from home. Even a year ago, they had still been close enough that he could distract her from her work with a neck massage, or an impromptu dance when her favorite song popped into the speakers from her playlist. Hopefully, those moments would happen again someday soon.

Because no matter what the past had held for them, or what the future promised, he still desired her.

He knelt on one knee by the sofa. "How are you feeling?"

"Exhausted, but cared for." She bit her lip before continuing, "I'd hoped meeting your family would spark memories, but no luck."

Guilt pinched, but it was best for all of them if she didn't remember right away.

Or ever.

He picked up her hand and held it loosely, keeping himself in check. How easy it would be to sit on the sofa and pull her into his lap. "Shana, I know this has to be awkward for you."

It had been so long since they'd shared that kind of ease.

"That's an understatement." Her eyes held his for a moment before she eased her hand away. She searched the room, her gaze never lingering long on any one spot. He followed her frenzied survey, taking in the bookshelves that arched high to the ceiling. Those shelves had been one of the things she'd loved most about this place, along with the greenhouse. He remembered how her face had lit up at the thought of a ladder leading to books wrapped around the room.

She showed no signs of remembrance on her face.

Giving her space—for now—he pushed to his

feet. "I want you to know I'll be sleeping in the guest room."

"Thank you. I realize this is tough for you, too."

"That's an understatement." He repeated her words, except for his own reasons. "But I know it's far worse for you. I want you to take your time, take care of yourself, and the baby."

"Thank you for understanding."

He was walking a tightrope, needing to give her space, but working with a ticking time bomb that meant she could remember their past at any moment.

For now, though, there was peace.

Since she was settled, this would be a neutral time to check on work without worrying about her getting angry at him.

He slid behind the desk and fired up his laptop, watching Shana out of the corner of his eye.

She shifted on the sofa and hugged a throw pillow over her stomach where their child was nestled, growing. "What are you working on?"

"Clearing away paperwork so I'll have more days off to spend with you."

"I'm not an invalid. And my mother will be here for a week." She tipped her head to the side. "Are you one of those guys who can't stand his mother-in-law?"

He weighed his words carefully as the truth could be tricky on this one. Her mom—Louise—had never seemed to warm to him. But then, she didn't trust many people. Life had left her overcautious.

"About four years ago your mother took a job in California." Louise was a civilian employed nurse at a military installation. "Most of the time, you visited her rather than having her coming back here."

"Hmm…" Shana seemed to digest the information, glancing around the library, her gaze lingering on the laptop and the stack of files. "I'm sorry to keep you from the office."

The words felt like a blow.

They'd had so many arguments over him being a workaholic. He didn't think of his work that way since he loved his job. He'd been groomed to take over for his parents once they retired, except retirement hadn't come. His father had died. His mother had doubled down, working to numb her grief. Only recently had she stepped back, since she'd fallen for her business rival. But now they were merging the oil companies.

It was a dangerous time for Chuck to take personal leave, but he didn't have much of a choice. His wife needed him, and he needed to win her back. For his own sake, and for the sake of their child.

Their family's future depended on it.

He felt the weight of her gaze on him and looked up.

Shana closed her book and reached for the mug of hot cocoa. "What's going on?"

"Why do you ask?" He clamshelled his laptop, looking directly at her.

She set aside her mug and hugged her knees to

her chest. "You look worried. I hate that I'm putting more stress on you. I know this has to feel even more awkward for you than it does for me."

He shook his head dismissively. "What makes you say that? You're the one who's lost five years."

"But I'm not the one whose spouse doesn't remember me. I know that has to hurt, and I'm so sorry."

She hugged her knees tighter, eyes locking with his. The heat rose between them in an undeniable connection, building like the crackling fire.

"I'm focused on what's best for you."

"Then what's got you so worried? I don't have to be a private detective to read the tension in you."

He creaked back in the office chair, deciding to share. "We've been struggling with data leaks for a while, trying to follow the trails in email exchanges."

"A mole in the company?" She uncrossed her legs and pushed herself off the couch. As she moved through the white room, her hands lingered on stray books on the coffee table. She walked to the fireplace and picked up a heavy crystal photo frame off the mantel—a picture of the two of them from a romantic train getaway, from Anchorage to the Arctic Circle. He'd been trying to cheer her up after a failed in vitro attempt.

"Seems so. We hired a new employee who, as it turns out, had a vendetta against us and the Steeles."

"What does the spy have to say?" She set the

frame down and drew closer. Lithe as ever. Hot as hell. She sank back into the sofa, curling up.

"She's disappeared somewhere in Canada." He righted his chair, then stood and walked toward her.

"And you've hired private investigators."

"Of course." He sat on the sofa, close enough that her toes grazed his thigh and the scent of her perfume tempted him to bury his face in her neck and inhale deeper. He recalled well how she always preferred floral scents in perfume, shampoo, even essential oils, all carrying through her love of flowers.

As much as he hated the unanswered questions at work, he welcomed the ease of being with Shana this way, without the anger of the past year that had torn their marriage apart.

"What do the investigators have to say about the data trails from her email exchanges?" she asked.

"Nothing."

"Nothing at all?" She shook her head. "That's strange."

"And you think you could do better."

"I surely couldn't do any worse."

He snorted on a laugh. "Fair enough. What are you proposing?"

"I don't know how I used to spend my time while we were married, but I will go stir-crazy just sitting around. Let me do my part and take a stab at finding this woman." She tapped his mouth before he could talk.

The feel of her fingers on him made him ache

to clasp her wrist and pull her onto his lap. Seal his mouth to hers and lose themselves in the way they connected best.

But pushing too far, too fast would only harm his cause. So he simply took her arm and pressed a kiss to her palm before lowering her hand. Her throat moved in a long swallow that sent a surge of victory through him.

"So, Shana, how do you want to proceed?"

"Have the human resources department send me her application and any other information on her. I'll start by digging around on the internet to see what I can find."

He wanted to wrap her in a cocoon, keep her close to protect her. Shana was strong-willed, and her fire had attracted him to her from the first.

But her fire, her determination, also made things tough right now. If he wasn't careful, she'd apply those investigative skills to their past.

Perhaps internet research would distract her from the amnesia, keep her from digging too deep into how things had been between them.

The last thing he wanted was for her to find out that on the day of her aneurysm, they'd decided to separate.

For the first time since waking up disoriented in the hospital room, Shana could finally breathe.

The warm shower sluicing down her back eased

her tensed muscles. The stress came as much from her too-sexy husband as it did from any medical issues.

If only she could hide in the shower forever, just let the water wash away all tensions, all concerns. She would pretend for just a moment her life was simple and uncomplicated as the scent of her shampoo mingled with the aroma from the floral-scented candle she'd lit.

How could she have forgotten her marriage? Had the aneurysm wiped five years from her mind for life? Or was the loss stress-related, not coincidental that the memory loss started at the time she'd met her husband?

Trust was difficult enough for her under normal circumstances. She slid her hand over her stomach.

There was no room for error. The stakes were too high. And she needed to take care of her health, which included rest.

She turned off the shower and stepped out onto the heated floor. A sigh of pleasure slipped free. She definitely didn't remember these, or any of the other luxuries from this life with Chuck Mega-Wealthy Mikkelson.

Except she was a Mikkelson now, too.

This was all too much to think about.

She should be relaxing. She tugged a towel free and dried off, then wrapped the fluffy cotton around her body. She squeezed water from her hair, making her way into the dressing area.

And slamming into a warm wall of hunky man.

Chuck.

Heat from the floor radiated up to send a flush of awareness through her body. Maybe it had been a bad idea moving in here with him as she waited for a cure for the amnesia. This kind of intimacy, the magnitude of their attraction, all of it so fast was… unsettling.

"Excuse me," he said, clasping her shoulders, his broad hands launching a tingle of excitement through her breasts. "I was just coming in to get some clothes from our closet."

Our closet.

She drew in a couple of steadying breaths. "I, uh…" Her mouth went dry. She clutched the towel in a fist between her breasts. She should step away.

Should.

"I'll leave you to it, then."

His thumbs moved along her collarbone. "I thought you were still downstairs in the kitchen."

The touch scrambled her thoughts and stole her breath.

"I feel bad kicking you out of your bedroom," she said, her eyes drawn to the vibrant green of his. "I can sleep in the guest room. It's not like I'll miss this space since I don't remember it being mine."

Theirs. Together.

Her gaze slid past him into the bedroom. How had they spent their time here before she'd become ill?

She looked up to the tray ceiling and toward the black fan. She felt disoriented, spinning and spinning, like the blades circulating heated air. She wondered if she'd ever stop circling around this awareness, this nagging feeling at the back of her mind.

She hated how she looked at the plush bed, with its overstuffed white pillows pressed against a headboard that practically went to the ceiling, and remembered…nothing.

This place felt foreign.

Even the pieces of her life that she recognized— like the antique perfume bottle from her grandmother on the mirrored bedside table—felt out of place. Familiar but not enough to comfort her.

She realized Chuck hadn't responded. His eyes had been tracking hers as she struggled to deal with this attraction to a man she barely knew.

"I feel bad that things are so awkward between us," she said.

"There's no instruction manual for how to deal with this."

She closed her eyes. Breathed in a hint of his aftershave, which sent a shiver through her that had nothing to do with the chilly day. She opened her eyes. "I've turned your life upside down."

"More like you're turning me inside out in that towel."

"Oh. Right. Sorry." Heat stung her face.

"You have nothing to apologize for. It's not your fault." His hands slid down her arms and then away from her body as he stepped back. "Good night, beautiful. Sleep well."

After the way his touch had felt?

Doubtful her night would be at all restful.

Chuck stretched back into the stiff off-white chair. He blinked his eyes clear, gearing up for another late night in his home office. The yellow light from the desk lamp dully illuminated the study.

He stacked Shana's things on the desk, putting her paperwork off to the left side, adjacent to the floral arrangements she'd picked out only four days ago.

Might as well have been in another lifetime.

The prospect of divorce rattled him.

Mikkelsons didn't fail.

He'd been unable to sleep after walking in on Shana coming out of the shower. Only a couple of days ago they'd been at each other's throats. Now, desire lit up the room every time they were near.

But he saw the wariness in her eyes. And truth be told, he wasn't interested in launching himself into the emotional shredder with her. He needed to save their marriage, but he also needed to keep things lighter between them. Surely they could enjoy the chemistry they shared and get back on an even footing in their relationship. Eventually, if this pregnancy came to term, they could also bring up their child.

Chuck shook his head, needing to focus. And not on Shana for the moment. For now, he needed to pay attention to the numbers on the chart in front of him and prepare for his late-night meeting.

He highlighted a few lines and scribbled thoughts off to the side. His messy handwriting populated the second page of the document. His eyes slid from the chart to his watch. 11:30 p.m.

Sure, it was an unconventional meeting time. But everything lately seemed mighty damn unconventional. He fired up his laptop and turned on another light in the office. He looked around at the space—his shared space with Shana—and could see all the memories. How she'd arranged the bookshelf first by genre, then by author. She loved reading. And he'd been happy to help her locate the perfect ladder, the perfect carpenter for the recessed bookshelves, the perfect table desk. A lifetime ago.

A lifetime he might have another shot at.

The ding of Broderick's conference call interrupted Chuck. Right. Business. Broderick's uncle Conrad was a night owl, too, so the late time didn't faze him, either. As for Chuck, he welcomed the chance to throw himself into work for a while, no matter the time. Broderick had set the time for after his daughter was asleep.

The video feed lurched to life, pixels turning smooth. Conrad and Broderick sat in the conference room at the Alaska Oil Barons, Inc., office, clean-cut and ready.

No Jack Steele this go-around. Just his second-incommand, Broderick, Jack's eldest son. And Jack's brother Conrad stepping in to consult.

Conrad Steele leaned forward, deep blue eyes a stark contrast to his thick salt-and-pepper hair. In his deadpan way, no emotions entering his expression, Conrad asked, "How're things with Shana?"

"Still no recollection of the past. But we're settling into a new routine." One full of desire that left Chuck aching. He wouldn't mention that. "I appreciate your accommodating my working from home."

Broderick nodded, brow tense as he leaned forward, too, setting a pen down on the dark wood conference table. "If you need time off, just say the word."

Chuck barked a laugh. Time off was the furthest thing from his mind. "Last time I took a month for personal reasons, my brother threatened to break my legs."

Conrad smiled tightly. "Trystan handled himself well with the press and at the fund-raiser."

Trystan was the younger Mikkelson brother, who had been adopted by Jeannie and her first husband after his mother, Jeannie's sister, had become addicted to drugs. He was as much a part of the family as all the other Mikkelson siblings.

"Other than punching the paparazzi." Broderick shot his uncle a look.

The older man shrugged. "Some would say the situation warranted a fist to the face."

Grinning, Chuck said, "And some would say you're siding with my brother to cause trouble."

Conrad steepled his fingers along his nose. "Trust between our families isn't going to happen in a day."

Hell yeah on that point. "Especially when people like Milla Jones are throwing around accusations about my family."

Chuck wondered what Shana might find once she dug into the former employee's files. Shana might have turned his life upside down, demanding more of Chuck than he knew how to give, but there was no denying she was all aces at her job. He wondered why he hadn't asked her to take this on before her accident. Maybe because she'd seemed to have given up on her career as an investigator to make time for her fertility treatments.

Maybe that was one of the mistakes they'd made as a couple.

Conrad creaked back in his chair. "You said it. Not me."

Silence descended. All three men exchanged looks, but no one spoke.

After what seemed like an eternity, Chuck shifted his weight forward, ready to make this conversation productive. "Shana's feeling at loose ends sitting around the house. I've asked her to look into Milla Jones's disappearance." As well as the woman's accusations about the Mikkelson family possibly being involved in the crash that killed Jack Steele's wife and daughter. Chuck hadn't shared the depth of the accusations with Shana yet. It had felt like too much to pile on her tonight.

And he hadn't wanted to taint her feelings about his family. About him.

Broderick crossed his arms over his chest, annoyance written all over his body. "We've dedicated unlimited resources to company investigators looking for Ms. Jones."

And they hadn't turned up a thing. "It doesn't hurt to have more eyes on the lookout. Shana is good at what she does. I should have thought to ask her earlier."

More than once, Shana had accused him of not supporting her work. In the early days of their marriage, he'd traveled so much on business it had started to take a toll on their relationship. He'd persuaded her to take a hiatus to travel with him. A few months had turned into a year and her position had been filled once she discussed returning. And then they'd turned their attention to starting a family.

Conrad spread his arms in surrender. "Well, by all means, if she can find Milla Jones, then I'm in. Whatever we can do to help her, we will."

"Thank you," Chuck said. "She'll need something to take her mind off losing her memory."

Conrad leaned forward on his elbows. "How are you?"

"Concerned," he admitted. "She's so damn stubborn."

A rustle from across the room caught his attention. A little noise, the sound of footfalls, the creak of a door hinge. He looked up and over, past the computer screen and into the depths of the ill-lit room.

Shana.

She stood at the door frame, blond hair loose.

But those eyes.

After being married to Shana for nearly four years, he knew that look all too well.

He was in the doghouse.

Four

Shana held herself in check by sheer force of will.

How. Dare. He.

Appease her? Placate her?

Lingering in the threshold to the home office—her *shared* home office—her blood boiled.

Did this man know her at all after five years together? And while she might still be locked out of her memories, she couldn't imagine that she had changed so much that any man—let alone her husband—would think she needed to be thrown a pity case to work on.

As if that would solve a damn thing.

Gripping the door frame, she felt her cheeks heat even more as she locked eyes with Chuck. The glow from the computer screen somehow made this broad-shouldered man seem impossibly Viking-like, with that squared jaw and stubble.

Her righteous anger at being thrown a case as a *distraction* was paralleled only by her anger at finding him so damn sexy.

She'd come downstairs for a snack in an attempt to feed her emotions that were still too tingly from their encounter outside the shower. Of course, that could also have something to do with why she couldn't keep herself from following the intoxicating timbre of his voice.

Too bad his words hadn't matched up to the allure.

Fury firing her steps, Shana crossed the threshold into the workspace, hugging her terry cloth robe tighter around her.

"You're just trying to pacify me?"

"Hold on, I need to sign off." Chuck looked back at the computer screen. "Conrad, Broderick, let me get back to you later." Closing the laptop, Chuck pushed up from the desk. "I'm not sure how much you overheard, but—"

"I heard enough to know you only asked me to help this investigation because you want to keep me busy—" she paused for a breath, anger making her dizzy "—not because you truly believe I have anything of value to offer."

Chuck took a beat, studying her face. Those green eyes shone in the dim room, bearing down into her soul. Awakening something…

But never mind that.

She crossed her arms over her chest in a challenge. No backing down.

"You want the truth? Fine." He walked around the corner of the desk and sat on the edge of it. "I want you to rest and to devote your energy to healing, for yourself and the baby. Can you imagine how awful it was to see you pass out and not be able to revive you?"

Anger seeped from her, replaced by an image that, even though she couldn't remember the event, she could still imagine clearly, and it tugged at her heart for him. "I'm sorry you went through that. But surely it crossed your mind that pregnant women pass out sometimes."

He stayed silent, his face sanitized of expression.

He was hiding something. God, she hated the inequality of him knowing *everything* while she stood in a void.

What would it have been like to meet him on even footing? The attraction between them was so intense.

And it was distracting her from reading the signs.

Something was off between them, and she needed to get to the bottom of it.

Her sleuthing skills screamed, an alarm walloping through her head. *Deep breaths*. She could figure this out. She had to, for the sake of her future here with this man. For the sake of her unborn child.

"You knew I was pregnant, didn't you? Or did you?" Her legs folded and she sat on the armchair near him as the truth became all too evident. "You didn't know about the baby. Why didn't I tell you?"

He scrubbed a hand along the back of his neck. "I suspect because of failed in vitro attempts and three miscarriages. You didn't want to get my hopes up."

"That makes sense." Yet it still felt like there was more to the picture when it came to why she would keep such news from him, from her husband.

"You sound skeptical."

"I sound like someone who doesn't know you well enough to form an opinion on whether you're trustworthy or not," she blurted out, head tilting as if to better take him in amid the books and flowers. She'd dreamed of a space like this when she was younger. Of course, younger felt like only a year or two ago—not six or seven years ago.

His jaw flexed, his lips thinning.

"You're angry." She stated the obvious, curious about why he'd had that reaction.

"I don't like my honor being called into question," he said tightly. "I just want what's best for you, for us."

Her own irritation was fanning back to life. "And that includes pacifying your baby's mother with busywork."

"I respect your professional instincts. I always have." He sounded sincere.

Still, she felt the need to press. "So I've been working during our marriage? Where's my business office?"

"You worked for the first year, until we decided to start a family."

She'd completely stepped away from the career she loved? Another twist, a blow she hadn't even considered. "I haven't worked in three years?"

"You did some consulting on occasion. And you organized incredible fund-raisers for the family." He gave her a roguish smile. "I have to tell you that if you dismiss the importance of that, there are women in our family who'll come after you."

"Your mother the business executive? Your sister the CFO? Or your stepsister the lawyer?" she retorted.

She refused to let his roguish smile throw her off the scent. She'd found a sensitivity and she needed to follow it.

He stood from the desk and knelt on one knee in front of her. "Are you trying to provoke me into an argument?"

"Is that what we used to do? Fight a lot?"

She wanted to spark some memory free, something tangible to hold on to from the past five years with this man she'd cared for—enough to marry him, to give up her career to try having children together.

He took her hand in his, his clasp steady, launching tingles up her arm. "I realize that losing your memory has to be…untenable. Finding out you're married, you gave up your job, must be so hard. Finding out you're carrying a child you don't recall conceiving is more than unfair." He palmed her stomach possessively. "But let me reassure you, I remember well when we made this baby."

Sliding his hand from her still-flat belly, he lifted her hand and pressed his mouth to her wrist. Her whole body flushed with a heat that rivaled the intensity she'd felt outside the shower. The sizzle of an almost-kiss, inhaling one another's breaths, their scent.

There was no question.

They shared a connection that had nothing to do with her pregnancy.

Chuck rocked back on his heels, stood and walked away, leaving her with more questions than answers.

Chuck had a sneaking suspicion he'd find Shana in the barn.

When they'd started dating, his parents' barn had been her favorite place. He recalled how she'd taken solace in the quiet caring of the horses, a natural horsewoman. He'd gotten her a fiery filly soon after they'd tied the knot, a bay Tennessee walking horse with a feathery mane. Her name was Sedna, after the Inuit goddess of sea animals.

Over the past four years, they'd spent time breaking the horse, transforming the leggy colt into a beautifully disciplined mare.

Unlike the barn of his professional enemy turned family, the Mikkelson family barn operated for business as well as for family recreation. The sleek steel

fifteen-stall structure featured small turnout pad-
docks and a climate-controlled tack room.

He walked down the spine of the building until he
reached the last stall on the right side. Sedna's stall.

Realizing the fight last night would not win Shana
over, Chuck knew he had to do better. He had to romance her. Because he'd been given a second chance
to regain the marriage he'd almost lost. And because
he needed to taste her lips and feel her body again.

So he'd gathered a bouquet of irises from their
hothouse. He held the flowers behind his back and
swept off his Stetson, hooking it on the back of a
post.

Biting wind whipped through the open door to
the small paddock behind Sedna's stall. Shana's
honeyed hair fanned around her, her cheeks chapped
from the cold.

It had taken all his willpower not to kiss her lips
last night. The velvety softness of her wrist had
nearly undone him.

She held a soft brush in her hand and seemed
to absently brush the horse. While the memory of
Sedna might not be available to her, his wife's ease
around horses remained.

An ease that had once allowed them to take a
weekend-long camping trek through the woods on
horseback during the summer. He'd always been
mesmerized by how Shana looked just as elegant in
jeans and boots as in an evening gown and jewels.

In the chill of the night, they'd warmed themselves with lovemaking. He could still hear the echo of her sighs, still feel the glide of her body. He'd held her in his arms afterward as the sun rose early in the summer months.

As if she could read his thoughts, Shana glanced over her shoulder. A question already formed in the tension of her brow.

He brought his arm from behind his back, his fist around the paper-wrapped irises from the greenhouse. Year-round flowers had been his first anniversary gift to her. "You wanted to know more about the past five years. These always made you smile."

A smile spread across her face now, her eyes lighting with pleasure as she took the flowers from him.

"Thank you. This is so thoughtful, but you don't have to buy me things." Still, she buried her face in the blossoms and inhaled.

"Consider it a first-date gift." Except this wasn't a date. "Or a first-full-day-home gift."

"They're gorgeous." She smiled over the bouquet, her blue eyes deepening with joy to a near purple echoed in the flowers. "Thank you."

"They're from the greenhouse."

Her eyebrows shot up. "We have a greenhouse?"

"I like the way you say 'we.'" He rested an elbow on the horse stall, his shoulder brushing hers.

Her smile faded. "That was presumptuous of me."

"Not at all." He angled closer, their knees grazing, his back blocking the wind rolling through the open barn door. "This is our home. This is where we've built our life together."

Her hands clenched in the paper, crackles echoing along with horse's whinnying. "Chuck—"

"No need to say anything." He toyed with a lock of her hair. How long had it been since he'd flirted with her? Too long. "I realize this is all new to you. Let me know how I can help."

"I want to know—I want to remember. I feel at such loose ends." She glanced up at him. "If you're still interested in my helping out in researching the missing employee, I *could* use something to occupy my time, especially until my mother arrives."

"I would very much appreciate your expertise in digging into Milla Jones's disappearance."

"Okay then. I'm all in. Even after my mom arrives." She looked down, their boots almost touching on the dusty barn floor. She shuffled her feet. "Do you and my mother get along?"

"Sure." He took the flowers from her and set them along the stall ledge.

"Care to elaborate?" She leaned back, arms across her chest.

Were her breasts swollen from pregnancy or was it his awareness that made them so appealing? Either way, he burned to test their weight in his hands.

His eyes grazed her chest before sliding up to her face. "Your mother and I don't argue."

"I guess I was looking for details on what you two talk about, or what you enjoy about each other."

He searched for something to share that wouldn't bring up her father. He knew she didn't like to talk about him. "Your mom makes my favorite cookies when she visits."

"What are your favorite cookies?" She went back to brushing Sedna. The horse shivered, swishing her tail lazily.

"Macadamia nut."

"Sounds delicious. Now I'm craving some."

"Craving?" His chest went tight.

She nodded, dropping her arm from brushing. "I guess that's a pregnancy thing."

He smiled and draped an arm around her shoulders.

She stiffened but didn't pull away.

"Do you mind my touching you?" He squeezed her shoulder lightly.

"I don't think so." She swayed toward him ever so slightly.

"A resounding endorsement," he said drily.

She let out a low laugh. A real, genuine one.

A surge of hope—and desire—filled him.

Laughing with her, teasing, felt good. But he was all too aware of how that laughter would stop if she remembered their more recent past before he had a chance to wrangle his way back into her bed again. Before he could reestablish the connection they had lost.

He was walking a tightrope, balancing savvy timing with racing against the clock.

One week and…nothing.

Not one memory bubbled to the surface. Nothing. Nada. Zilch.

Shana had tried holding items throughout the house. Smelling them. And still not one memory came.

She trudged forward on her daily walk, snowshoes crunching the packed surface. The crisp air teased her lungs and senses, but she couldn't shake the frustration of still feeling like an interloper in her own life.

The Mikkelson and Steele families were all visiting today. Not one person in the sea of faces managed to dislodge a memory from its hiding place.

Closing the last few steps to the house, she puffed free a cloud of air. She knelt and removed her snowshoes, one, then the other. Holding them, she opened the side porch door into the mudroom, relishing the quiet before descending into the chaos that was her new normal. So many people—relative strangers—hovered over her, staring at her with expectant eyes.

Her mom had never made it. After having had her flight canceled multiple times for weather, she'd decided to wait until later to visit rather than risk using up all her vacation days for a trip that might not happen.

Shana was on her own to sort through her convoluted life.

Glenna, Chuck's elegant sister, had invited Shana on a snowshoe walk through the grounds. His eldest sister seemed warm and thoughtful. She'd married the eldest Steele brother, Broderick. So many names still.

Glenna had popped back inside to check on her child, leaving Shana in the mudroom between the family inside the house and outside. Hand on her stomach, Shana let her eyes flutter closed.

She'd worked off some of her tension from being in close quarters with her sexy husband, who'd been Prince Charming personified every minute of every day. He hadn't been pushy, and that made him somehow all the more alluring. Every accidental touch and thoughtful gift had her tied up in knots.

He'd made dinner himself the other night. Chuck dug up her mother's Alfredo recipe and served it complete with a dark chocolate mousse cake—which he didn't bake, but had special ordered for her. So kind. And yet so strange.

He'd finished off the meal with the gift of a bracelet holding a studded diamond charm.

Her eyes fluttered back open, away from recent, accessible memories to the unfolding present. She looked for her husband through the mudroom window. A combination of snowmobiles and horses disrupted the snow-covered land, white-capped mountains in the distance.

There was a pristine beauty around the five acres of property. Chuck had told her his stable was small compared to the Steele spread, and his family kept things more understated. Somehow, as if by practice, she immediately located Chuck on his stallion Nanook—a buckskin quarter horse.

Chuck looked natural. Rugged. Familiar and strange.

She'd made it through the first week under the same roof as her husband. Although that didn't stop her from thinking about him all the time.

Of course, that could be in part because the pillows carried a hint of his scent. She hadn't been able to resist inhaling, wondering if the smell would bring memories of him or memories of when they'd conceived the baby she carried.

How surreal to be pregnant. She didn't feel different other than her breasts were a little tender. Yet the ultrasound was real, as was the follow-up appointment with her doctor yesterday. She was responsible for caring for the life growing inside her.

Chuck had mentioned several miscarriages and unsuccessful fertility treatments. Her pregnancy, combined with the amnesia, had to be all the more difficult for him.

How long would it take for her to remember?

Desperately needing to connect with something familiar, she reached into her coat pocket for her cell phone to call her mother. She craved stability. She clicked the phone on Speaker as she made her way into the kitchen.

No, *her* kitchen. The kitchen she clearly had a hand in decorating.

She listened to the ringing phone, eyes investigating the three suspended lamps that illuminated a white marble counter free of any clutter. Her actual dream.

Or rather, her lived reality.

Walking to the island, she smelled the bouquet of irises, another endearing gesture from Chuck. Turning, she opened the freezer and pulled out a tub of home-churned berry ice cream, a craving she'd had that Chuck made sure stayed in good supply, along with extra berries to spread on top.

After what felt like an eternity of ringing, the phone clicked on just as she pulled a spoon out from the drawer.

"Hello there, sweetie. I'm so sorry not to have made it. I'm going to save up all my vacation days to get there as soon as I can. But it could be a month or so."

Shana stifled the urge to beg her mom to come anyway. But she needed to be strong and learn to stand on her own in case things didn't work out with Chuck. "I'm okay, Mom. Really. Chuck's whole family is watching out for us."

"But I'm your mama." Evident pain passed through the phone. Shana scooped up a bite of berry ice cream before she answered, savoring the bitter notes of the blackberries.

Shana wanted to agree with her mother, but guilting her mom wouldn't help. "I understand, truly I do."

"I worry about you being there with them all feeling like strangers to you."

True enough. Her whole life felt surreal. "It's awkward at times, but they're being sensitive."

"And Chuck? How is he?"

Sexy. Unreadable. But thoughtful. And… "Careful."

He treated her like she was fragile and could break at any moment. She hated that.

"Careful doesn't tell me much."

"He's walking on eggshells trying to make me happy."

"That should be a good thing."

Except when someone had an agenda.

Pressing her palms into the countertop, Shana drew in a breath, then let it out. She scanned the pristine kitchen as if it held a clue.

Maybe it did.

The words smoked through her mind and under her defenses. Her imagination ran wild from her days as a private eye. Days on the job had showed her the dark secrets people like her father hid, people who many would think were everyday, regular folks.

Goose bumps prickled. Shana searched for a way to end the call. Her mother had suffered too much. Shana didn't want to add more worries, especially when there might well be nothing to be concerned about.

If there was ever a need for superior detective skills, it was now. Shana needed to piece together what had happened over the past five years. Fast.

"Hmm." She wasn't ready to tell her mother about the baby. Her life already felt so alien and unsure. She would tell her mom in person once she arrived. "Hey, I hear someone calling for me, so I'll let you go."

"Call me anytime. Love you, sweetie."

"Love you, too, Mom." She ended the call, no closer to finding answers, and only filled with more burning questions.

She scooped more ice cream into her mouth and shut her eyes again. In the movies, characters were always shutting their eyes to remember long-forgotten secrets. More than a week without any hint of her past and she found herself ready and willing to try anything.

An arm slid around her shoulders. Instant heat tingled in her skin from that strong weight.

How quickly she'd come to recognize his touch.

Chuck. Her husband.

She looked over her shoulder to smile and offer him a spoonful. "Want some?"

"Hmm." He grinned and opened his mouth.

She fed him the ice cream, shivers running up her arm. She hadn't thought about how sexy sharing food would be, but now? Her body melted faster than the serving in her bowl.

She cleared the lump in her throat—easier said than done. "How was your ride?"

He swept off his Stetson and set it on the granite counter. "Mind-clearing."

"Did we ride together often?"

He stroked back her hair, strands catching along his calluses. "We did. And we will again."

The words hung between them with the promise of a future she couldn't quite envision. Living in the present with a chunk of the past gone was tough enough.

His smile faded into a frown and she realized he was looking over her shoulder.

She touched his arm lightly. "Is something wrong?"

"I'm not sure." He leaned forward, hands on the counter, looking through the window. "But it sure seems like my baby sister is getting cozy with the youngest Steele kid."

"Kid? They look like adults to me."

"Freshmen in college." He swept his hat off the counter. "And since my and Alayna's mom married Aiden Steele's dad, those two freshmen are living under the same roof."

He jammed his Stetson back on his head and stalked out the door.

As she watched Chuck storm across the yard, leaving a trail of footprints in the snow, she fought back the unsettling feeling that this man bore little resemblance to her careful husband of the past week.

Alayna Mikkelson hugged Aiden Steele as he powered the snowmobile across the pristine stretch of ice left after the storm. She wrapped her arms tighter around one of the hottest college freshmen on campus and her brand-new stepbrother.

Even through the puffy snow gear, she could smell Aiden's clove aftershave, a rich scent, as dark and mysterious as his hair and eyes. The kind of eyes that induced blushes on even the most popular fresh-man girls. But here she was, perched on the back of a snowmobile with him.

They weren't blood-related. And her mom hadn't even been married to his dad for a year. So there was nothing creepy about her feelings for him. He prob-ably wouldn't have noticed her on campus. But liv-ing in the same house with her over the past months, somehow he'd *seen* the real her.

When so many others didn't.

Being the quiet one in her family had its down-sides, like when she went unnoticed or got steam-rolled. But being quiet also had its perks, like hearing all the juiciest gossip because people tended to over-look wallpaper personalities.

And the best perk right now? No one seemed to realize she was on her way to being majorly noticed by Aiden Steele.

She swallowed, eyes looking past his broad shoulders and to the distant horse-filled pastures. A thump in the ground pushed her forward, closer to Aiden. Her stomach did a somersault.

Life was so surreal these days with all the past family rivalries disappearing. Who would have thought they'd be having all these get-togethers after so many years of outright warfare?

She hadn't always been the kind of person to fade into the background. As a kid, she'd demanded her rights in a big family. Sometimes loudly.

How ironic that one event had changed her so radically, silenced her so completely.

She hadn't even started school when she'd over-heard Uncle Lyle—her mom's brother—talking to some strange men. To this day she couldn't recall exactly what she'd heard. She only knew it had been bad enough for him to threaten her. He'd said if she talked he would throw her through the ice and every-one would think she'd drowned. Once she'd gotten old enough to realize she should have told someone, he'd already disappeared from their lives. So there was nothing to be gained from sharing something that was now only a fuzzy memory.

Maybe she should be more proactive in digging up those memories. If she didn't, she might be for-ever stuck in the role of a wallflower. That kind of anonymity wasn't as comforting as it had once been.

Especially not when she wanted Aiden to see her.

Hanging around with Shana could be helpful on a number of levels. Seeing how professionals helped her regain her memories could provide tips on how to root around in Alayna's own buried recollections. Shana also happened to be a private detective and might have tips for finding out the truth of the past.

Nobody talked about Shana's career much since it seemed like everyone else either worked for the family oil business or planned fund-raisers.

There was no room for anything in between.

Even if Alayna decided to work for her family's empire someday, she needed that to be her decision.

She needed to find her voice again first.

And she needed to find a way to tell them what she knew, something deep down inside she'd feared would turn her family inside out.

Was this what Shana felt like without her memory? Afraid?

Alayna clutched Aiden harder. He would probably think it was because they'd shot over a pile of packed snow.

She knew her world had felt unsteady for a lot longer than just today.

Five

Anger coursed through Chuck's veins.

When he'd seen Alayna and Aiden together, instinct had fired his feet into motion. He hadn't even bothered to grab a jacket from the entry hallway of his home. Luckily, he hadn't yet removed his snow boots.

He heard Shana following after him. Worried she might slip on the ice, he slowed his pace and glanced over his shoulder to see her chasing him.

That chest-tightening feeling came back as he looked at her. Her puffed steel-gray jacket still managed to hug her curves and call attention to her hot figure. Her honeyed hair fell in waves, contrasting with her wind-chapped cheeks and lips. Genuine concern welled in those soft eyes.

Damn. A helluva mess.

Chuck knew full well he was channeling a week's worth of frustration into the moment. But damn it, his shy baby sister didn't need to get tangled up with one of the Steele men.

"Chuck? Take a breath." Shana's urgent voice floated over his shoulder. "Think about what you're doing." She leaned forward, hands pressing into her thighs.

"I'm putting a stop to this before it's out of hand." He eyeballed the snowmobile in the distance where Alayna was still plastered against Aiden Steele's back.

Shana drew closer and clutched his arm. "It could be a harmless flirtation."

"I beg to differ." He rested his hand over hers because, what the hell, he wasn't ever so far gone as to miss out on a chance to touch her. "My baby sister— my shy, innocent baby sister—is all over that hellion Steele kid."

"Seriously? You're worried because they're riding a snowmobile together?" She patted his arm. "And who says the guy's a hellion?"

"She doesn't need to sit that close, he doesn't need to let her, and he looks like trouble." His protective urges kicked into overdrive. While the family companies might have merged, while their families might be blended by marriage, none of that did much to alleviate years' worth of mistrust. Not even close.

She took both of his hands, clasping them in that calming way she'd done over the years of their marriage, like when his father had died.

"Chuck, you may be right on every point, but do you think confronting them will accomplish anything positive?"

Damn it, he hated that she was right. But he also couldn't deny an easing of his tension thanks to her perspective. He appreciated how kind she'd been to come after him when she didn't even remember any of them in the first place.

"What do you suggest?" he asked. "I can't just ignore what I see and send them both on their merry way to live under the same roof. What if he takes advantage of my little sister?"

"Maybe she plans to take advantage of him." She grinned, squeezing his hands.

"You're not helping."

"Fair enough. How about let me talk to her?" She nudged his shoulder.

A familiar gesture that should feel so damn normal. Except it had been a long time since he'd had a positive connection with his wife.

Was this a sign of life in their marriage?

"And you'll tell me what she says?"

Shana hesitated, then said, "I'll tell you if I think there's cause for concern."

She arched up on her toes and kissed him. A slight

brush of her lips to his, but a kiss that lingered for a moment too much to be anything platonic. The chemistry between them sparked like static popping in the air. He ached to haul her to him, her body flush against his. Yet patience would gain him so much more.

As she eased away, her eyes went wide. "I'm not sure why, um, I wasn't thinking, I, well…"

He pressed a finger to her soft lips. "No explanation needed."

Savoring the progress, he backed away, the taste of her filling him with victory.

Several days may have passed, but it didn't dull this particular memory.

She'd kissed Chuck.

On impulse but not by accident.

As much as she tried to keep her mind on the present and her conversation with Alayna, Shana found her mind wandering. Not that the teen seemed to notice as she chattered on about the gala next month. The event would gather the Alaska Oil Barons, Inc., shareholders and board members in a show of solidarity and celebration. The massive event was being planned by a Mikkelson distant cousin—Sage Hammond. Until now, Sage had been solely a personal assistant. She'd been given the event to prove herself and possibly advance in the company. So far, her work looked promising.

The gala had a steampunk theme blending Old

West fashion with a technology aesthetic, the perfect showcase for an oil company with Alaskan roots.

This was as good a way as any to learn how to navigate among the Mikkelsons. Or rather, *re*learn, as they seemed quite comfortable coming and going in her home. Chuck's sister Glenna sat off to the side on a blanket with her daughter, while his youngest sister, Alayna, curled up in a wing chair by the fire.

Seeing Chuck grow so tense earlier in the week over his sister's possible love life felt oddly endearing. He cared so much. But Shana remembered being a teenager, too. She knew that explosions and sharp decrees didn't necessarily assuage puppy love. No, affairs of the heart demanded a more tender touch.

Besides, Alayna's troubles could provide some diversion from Shana's own missing memory. Something about jumping in full force to the family dynamic appealed to her.

Shana touched the marble mantel, mindlessly arranging the large group of flowers in front of the towering mirror. She loved the opulent arrangement of ferns and gardenias. The brightness contrasted well with the white room. Greens, particularly ferns, always seemed hopeful and tenacious.

When Shana had been a child, her mother had read her a book about a magical princess who rekindled the land by restoring life to a resurrection fern. Her mom told her resurrection ferns were real. They really could survive and come back after great lengths of time without sustenance. Even as a small child, Shana had felt a kinship to the plant. She liked to care for the miracle ferns in her home.

Chuck's home.

Her sexy husband, Chuck.

The man who was both familiar to her and intoxicatingly new. A man she'd impulsively kissed.

Before her accident, would that kiss have rocked through her just as much? Were they a couple who stole intimate moments like that?

She had so many unanswered questions. She needed to touch him again, to feel him press into her body. She had to go back for more. Maybe, just maybe, another kiss could unleash more than the electricity that hummed in her bones every time they locked eyes.

Alayna cleared her throat after glancing over her shoulder as if to determine if her elder sister, Glenna, would be able to hear them—but Glenna was still engrossed with her baby daughter, who was playing with a jingling ball.

Shana shifted her attention back to Alayna.

One crisis at a time. That lingering kiss with Chuck would have to wait.

Forcing the memory of his lips from her mind, Shana tilted her head to the side. Alayna again looked back at her older sister. Glenna's blond hair was gathered into a high ponytail as she played with her baby girl. An array of stuffed animals and teething toys speckled the light lavender blanket.

Shana saw an opportunity. Her memory and the

specifics of this family might be gone, but her sleuthing skills were as sharp as ever. She still knew how to read people. Alayna clearly had something she wanted to share, and something she didn't want her older sister to know.

"Alayna, thank you for coming by the hospital to see me and spending time with me here."

Alayna shrugged, her oversize sweatshirt falling slightly off her shoulder. "You've been a sister to me for years. You helped me with picking makeup and dating. We were close."

"So we talked about boys."

Alayna blushed. "We did. Or rather the lack of boys in my life. I'm so shy, dating is tough for me."

A twinge went through Shana's heart. "Dating is tough for anyone in their teens and twenties... Honestly, relationships are tough when you're an adult, too."

"I'm sure amnesia doesn't help," Alayna said with eyes full of sympathy.

"I have so many questions."

"I'm glad to help how I can." Alayna paused, staring off in the distance. "Maybe you can help me with something, too."

"What would that be?"

Alayna chewed at her bottom lip, her eyes full of shadows. Whatever she wanted to talk about seemed to be weighing heavily on her. She looked away for a moment, then back with an overbright smile.

"Will you help me with my fashion sense?"

That wasn't the sort of request Shana had been expecting. It felt like a dodge. "I thought you already had a gown chosen for the gala."

"I do, but that's more of a costume since it's got the whole steampunk theme. I'm talking about the day-to-day kind of stuff. And regular special events, like a rodeo."

Intrigued, Shana sensed Alayna was circling closer to her deeper concern. The rodeo sounded specific, like a place she planned to see someone she wanted to impress.

"Of course, I'm happy to help. But are you sure there's not something else you want to talk about?"

Alayna shook her head quickly. "Nope. It's just tough stepping out of the shadow of my mom and older sister. You're not quite as…um, well…pushy."

"I think you're lovely."

Alayna crossed her arms over her body, swimming in the oversize sweatshirt. The young woman looked down at her feet, shaking her head from side to side. "I want to be a knockout."

"Is there a guy in the picture?"

"I'm nineteen. Guys are all I think about."

"I do remember that time of life very well." Shana angled closer, their bodies effectively turned away from Glenna. "Now tell me about you and Aiden Steele."

A rush of scarlet colored Alayna's cheeks.

Here.

This was the opportunity she'd been waiting for.

Only, the window for sharing evaporated before her eyes. Alayna opened her mouth to reply but inhaled sharply as her mother, Jeannie, approached from the hall.

Shana felt her sister-in-law turn rigid as she mumbled, "I'm going to help Glenna change the baby's diaper. She deserves a break."

Just like that, Alayna moved as quickly as an Alaskan dogsled team cutting through the ice.

Jeannie's silvery-blond hair feathered around her face as she walked closer. "Teenagers," she laughed lightly. "It's hit or miss on when she wants my attention." Jeannie patted a pillow on the sofa. "You should take it easy. Put up your feet."

"I'm following the doctor's orders to the letter."

"That doesn't stop me from worrying."

"I understand." Shana paused, wondering if there was a way to help the mother and the daughter. Clothes shopping had a way of soothing a teenage soul. "Alayna asked me to go shopping with her for something to wear to the rodeo. Would you like to come along? We could all have lunch together."

"That sounds delightful." Her mother-in-law smoothed her hair before continuing, "Are you sure my daughter won't mind?"

"Why should she?"

"Asserting her independence has made things prickly between us."

Even from the brief time she'd known this family, Shana could see how tight the Mikkelsons were.

They were there for each other. And yes, that felt a little claustrophobic to her at times, especially growing up as an only child, but she also couldn't deny she'd once wanted something like this. "I can tell she loves you."

"I don't doubt that. It's just a stage of life, and I'm trying not to push it. Certainly my remarriage didn't help ease the path."

Now that the subject of Jeannie's marriage to Jack Steele had come up, it seemed a good time to mention the budding romance between the two teens living under the same roof. While Shana had initially been reticent to share details with Chuck, upon further reflection, it seemed wise to bring up the matter with Jeannie.

Shana placed the throw pillow on the glass coffee table and propped up her feet. Maybe if she focused on the teen's love life, she could stop thinking about her own convoluted relationship.

Even after supper, long past when his family had left, Chuck couldn't shake the memory of the tender fullness of Shana's lips on his, which was crazy. She was his wife of four years. They'd kissed more times than he could count.

But that brief brush—at her instigation—had moved him like no kiss he could remember.

He'd tried to put it out of his mind all day. To no use. Shana's touch burned deep into him, reawakening all of their years together—the good years when their love had been flame-hot.

Chuck pulled two antique bowls from the cabinet. They'd been his grandmother's. Shana always admired the divots in the purple Depression glass. He'd secured them from Glenna for a Valentine's Day gift for his wife three years ago.

Passing a bowl to Shana now, he wondered what item would tip her memory. When would they open the Pandora's box of their past, their complications?

But for now, she looked at the bowl only with admiration, like she was taking it in for the first time. Those light fingers touched the rim gingerly.

Shana glanced up at him through those thick lashes.

God, she looked gorgeous in leggings and a silky blouse, one hip leaning against the counter. Casual or glammed up, she always took his breath away.

He caught himself and moved toward the freezer. A few hours ago, he'd ordered more fresh-churned ice cream, this time lemon, determined to keep her as satisfied as possible.

He set the ice-cream container on the kitchen island adjacent to the blueberries, raspberries and blackberries. Shana fished spoons out from the nearby drawer and handed one to him, their fingers brushing ever so slightly.

Reminding him again of the sensation of her lips. The curve of her back.

As if that memory had, in fact, wound its way to

the forefront of Shana's mind, too, he noticed a faint blush rise and spread in her cheeks. There was something oddly comforting in her reaction.

He scooped lemon ice cream into her bowl, then his. Cradling his bowl in his hand, he leaned by her still-thriving bouquet, his knee brushing Shana's leg.

She spooned an extra helping of berries on her ice cream. "I wanted to reassure you about your sister. The opportunity arose to talk about the situation with your mother."

"What did Mom have to say?" He was still edgy and worried about Alayna. Of all of them, she'd been especially lost since their father died.

Shana looked down at her bowl. "Your mother said that Alayna and Aiden are both over eighteen, but since they're living under her roof, she'll keep watch and make sure they understand the ground rules of her house."

Some of the tension eased from him. He wasn't completely reassured, but at least his mother could keep an eye out. "That sounds like my mom."

Shana swallowed the spoonful of ice cream, the tip of her tongue swiping at the corner of her mouth in a tempting sweep. "So you approve of how I handled it?"

"I trust you." He'd always trusted her. It was Shana who'd come to the marriage with deep issues about trust, issues that had driven a wedge deeper between them with each passing year.

She stared into her bowl, quiet for too long.

Ah, that damn *trust* word.

Even without her remembering their marriage, this was still a sticking point between them. "I understand that trust is difficult for you because of your father."

Clutching the bowl with both hands, she adjusted her weight. He noted the tension in her jaw. Pain seemed to paint her slender face as a forced smile dusted her lips. "That's putting it mildly."

Maybe with the clean slate of her lost memories he could make some headway on this subject, handle it better than they had in the past. He covered her hand with his. "Your father is one person."

Her lips thinned. "One amoral person who completely fooled my mother and me for so long."

He linked his fingers with hers, and she didn't pull away. Promising. "I want to be understanding."

"Because I'm pregnant. You don't want me to leave with your child."

Damn, she was sharp. And too close to the truth for comfort.

He chose his words carefully. "So let me get this straight. Your father was dishonorable. And I'm in trouble for being honorable."

She pulled her hand away. "I would never take your child from you or keep you from seeing each other. If this pregnancy comes to term and we find we can't live together, I would work with you to put a plan in place for coparenting."

He could see her agitation in the way she mashed

the berries in the bowl. The last thing he wanted was to put stress on her. He couldn't take another health scare like the one they'd just been through. "Fair enough."

Tension faded from her body. "Thank you. Let's focus on my helping you find the employee from your company who went missing. You want me to look into things, but you keep delaying the start of my investigation."

"I just want to make sure you've recovered."

"The doctors say I'm fine. I feel fine. You should know. You were at my checkup." She smiled, her blue eyes sparkling more than the most valuable jewels. "Now, let's talk."

"The missing employee—"

"Milla Jones," she verified, "who disappeared somewhere in Canada—"

"Yes, her. Before she disappeared, she made it clear she was against the merger going through. She also said she wasn't the only one spilling secrets. There was a traitor in our family—on the Mikkelson side." The sweet taste of ice cream palled on his tongue at the thought of that accusation being in any way true. "This traitor supposedly played a part in the plane crash that killed Jack Steele's first wife and his daughter Breanna. What's worse, the Jones woman intimated that Breanna Steele was actually still alive."

She gasped. "What a horrible thing to say if it's

not true. How awful to give the Steeles hope that way."

"After the crash, the Steeles ran DNA tests from teeth found at the wreckage. The tests came back a match to Breanna's. Additional tests were run since she had a twin—Naomi Steele Miller." He thought of how much he and Shana wanted a child and how devastating a loss like that would be, a wreckage so fiery that identification came down to teeth.

Protectiveness surged through him. He would move heaven and earth to keep his wife—his family—safe.

She rubbed her forehead. "What would lead this Milla person to make up something like that, then?"

He fought the urge to massage her shoulders. Or ease the tension in a more pleasurable way.

"There are any number of reasons she could manufacture a story like that. To cause trouble. To drive a wedge between the families so the merger falls through. My first guess would be she was paid by a rival who stands to benefit."

"Such as?" she pressed, shifting against the counter, drawing his eyes to the slim length of her legs.

"Johnson Oil." The obvious answer. Johnson Oil was their main competitor in Alaska. "Before the merger, we were all on even footing competitively. Johnson is no match to the merged Alaska Oil Barons, Inc., though. If we pull this off, it's going to be a boon."

"Big business." She crinkled her nose.

"No need to sound so disdainful. It's not like

we're the only game in town. But this edge will give us the capital for innovation—such as Royce Miller's eco-friendly upgrades to the pipeline."

They'd brought on premier research scientist Royce Miller to implement new safety measures. In the process, he'd fallen in love with Naomi Steele. They had twin girls now. Apparently, twins ran in the Steele family.

"I get that your family and the Steeles are good people. And I'm working on trust, but it's tough flying blind here. I wish my mother hadn't been stuck in the airport so long for weather."

As much as he regretted seeing Shana's frustration, he couldn't deny he'd been relieved that her mother couldn't make the trip. Having Shana all to himself gave him the time he needed to pursue his quest to get her back into his bed, and secure a place in her life. Secure their future as a family.

He didn't intend to waste an instant.

The time for waiting to make a move was over.

He spooned up some lemon ice cream and offered it to her. "Try mine."

And before the night was out, he intended to taste *her.*

Six

Shana opened her mouth for the spoon, anticipation humming through her body at the intimacy of Chuck feeding her. His green eyes glimmered with promise as his gaze held hers.

What was it about this man that drew her so? Had the attraction between them always been this intense? Or was this a phantom memory due to the longevity of their relationship?

She tasted the ice cream, her senses on overdrive. The cream and berries burst along her taste buds, saturating her craving yet somehow leaving her yearning for more. More of this moment. More of him.

She wanted to accept the promise of a kiss in

his eyes. To follow wherever it led with no worry or regrets.

Chuck dipped the spoon back into his bowl. "This is like when we were dating."

She watched him take a taste from the silverware he'd just fed her with, unable to remove her gaze from him. "I wish I remembered."

"You will," he said confidently.

She wished she shared his certainty. She wasn't sure how she would trust in the future with such a gaping hole in her past. "And if I don't?"

"Let's work on new memories, here and now." Chuck angled closer, whispering in her ear. "I have an inside track here, knowing what you like."

He pressed his mouth against her neck, just over her leaping pulse. The heat of his breath fanned an answering warmth to life in her. His lips traveled to her collarbone. He nudged aside the neckline of her sweater for fuller access, each brush of his lips more tantalizing than the one before. Her hands clenched into fists as she held back the urge to grab him.

Instead, she lost herself in the sensations he stirred. His mouth grazed back to her neck, then up further to nip her earlobe. He kissed her ear, taking his time. Her head lolled to the side, giving him space.

Finally, thank goodness, his lips moved to hers. Except he didn't make contact. He just stayed a whisper away, his mouth hovering over hers.

Hunger gnawed at her.

Just as she swayed forward, he pulled away.

"That's not fair," she protested, her words riding a sigh of desire.

But maybe pulling back was what she needed. She wanted to trust he wasn't like her father. Getting to know Chuck better was a step in the right direction.

"You know just how to kiss me to turn me inside out. Yet I don't know much about you."

He spread his arms wide. "I'll willingly donate my body for your research."

She took in the leanly muscular length of him. "I just feel we're on uneven ground because of my amnesia."

He angled back, stroking aside her hair but also giving her space. "Judging by the way you kissed me, it felt like you know me, too, on some level."

"But on so many others, I don't." She stirred her spoon through the ice cream. "There's a part of me that wonders what you would do if I gave in to the temptation to kiss you now. Would we simply kiss while you respected my need for space, or would we both throw caution to the wind?"

"As much as I want to make love to you, I hear your reservation. I respect it. We're going to take our time." His voice held a promise echoed in his eyes.

"How much time?"

She wasn't sure what she wanted his answer to be. Part of her longed to find out what it would be like to spend the night in his arms. In his bed.

What if passion unlocked her memories?

But the rational side of her knew that giving in now, before she knew everything she needed to know, probably wasn't wise.

"As much time as you need." He kissed her lips lightly, nudging the bowl of ice cream toward her. "Good night, Shana."

Alayna kept her eyes on her bowl of caribou stew and off Aiden across the dinner table from her. And she feared her mother and her stepfather might notice her nerves, or worse yet, notice her interest. They had some convoluted notion of making them all a family, as if that was miraculously achieved by just sitting in the kitchen together for a meal rather than in the formal dining room.

Sighing, she stirred her stew in hopes no one would question her silence. She wasn't ready to share her feelings for Aiden with them yet, and maybe that had something to do with the fact she knew they wouldn't approve. Her brother sure didn't. She could tell.

Picking apart her yeast roll, she half listened to the drone of her mom and Jack talking about visiting Shana and Chuck. Aiden was just as quiet, although she was in tune to every clink of his spoon against the bowl. She snuck a look at him through her eyelashes.

No one else sat at the lengthy kitchen table even though it seemed half the world lived under this roof. Jack Steele had built this huge place with private suites for his kids, the size of luxury apartments. Her sister, Glenna, lived here now, married to Jack's son.

Which made it all the more ironic she was getting flack over hanging out with Aiden. She felt his eyes on hers.

He grinned at her wryly.

She struggled to keep from blushing as she grinned back. He jerked his head toward the door. Could he really be asking her to leave with him?

Her heart leaped into her throat. She nodded quickly. He held up a finger, indicating she should wait. Aiden pushed back his chair, placed his dishes in the sink, and made a beeline for the mudroom.

Conversation at the table stopped and Alayna's breath hitched in her throat. Her stepfather scraped his chair back, standing and following his son.

Disappointment stung. It shouldn't be this tough getting time alone together, given they lived in the same house. Frustrated, she pulled her linen napkin from her lap and tossed it beside her bowl to leave.

Jeannie rested a hand on her wrist. "Hold on a minute. Let's talk."

Something in her mother's voice set off alarms. She eyed her mom warily. "About what?"

"You and Aiden."

Her stomach knotted. "There's no me and Aiden." She felt compelled to ask, though, "But what if there were? How's that any different from Glenna and Broderick?"

Her mother rubbed between Alayna's shoulder

blades. "No need to get defensive. I simply want to make sure no one's heart gets hurt...and that no one ends up with a pregnancy before they're ready."

"Mom," she growled, shooting to her feet. "I get that you have to go all adult on me, but I'm nineteen. Trust me."

Heat rushed to her face. She wasn't used to speaking out this way and it made her uncomfortable. Not enough to take back the words.

In fact, as she raced back to her room, she was more determined than ever to find a chance to meet with Aiden. Alone.

Walking away from Shana the day before had been tough, but Chuck knew waiting for the right moment to make his move was crucial. He didn't want her to run. The stakes were too high.

He wasn't going to risk her walking out of his life.

For a second time.

Although the waiting was damn near killing him. Would tonight—their fourth anniversary—be that perfect moment?

He hoped so.

He had spent the day working on plans while she stayed at the computer, pensive. He'd given her space, easy enough since he'd had his hands full pulling off the perfect evening to go with the gift he'd bought for the occasion. She'd seemed pleased with the diamond heart bracelet he'd given her, so he'd decided to contact one of his mother's favorite jewelry designers, a Texas-based company called Diamonds in the Rough. They specialized in rustic, eclectic pieces. He was also having a special piece designed just for her for the gala celebrating the completion of the merger forming Alaska Oil Barons, Inc. She'd been a fan of their jewelry before the accident so he felt confident in his choice to shower her with pieces now.

After jogging down the stairs, he made his way to their home office, taking a beat outside the door to pat his suit jacket over where he'd tucked the gift. Shana sat at the desk, typing away on the keyboard while classical guitar music played softly through the sound system. She'd crossed her legs on the chair, a nearly empty glass of milk on the table reminding him of the child she carried. Their child.

Her fuzzy, soft sweater hugged the curves of her breasts, making his hands ache to touch her. But he'd told her he would respect her need for space and he would honor that.

A lot of bad had happened between them over the years, but he was determined to shield her from a repeat of their arguments. He would devote the same drive he had at the office to winning his way back into her bed and into her life.

As if she felt his gaze, she glanced up from the computer. "You look nice. Do you have a business meeting?" She glanced back at the screen. "It's pretty late, though. A dinner meeting, maybe?"

"A date, actually, with my wife."

"Well, since I'm craving burgers and a milkshake, you're a bit overdressed." She laughed, combing her fingers through her loose, honey-blond hair. Her bare ring finger served as a reminder she still hadn't totally embraced their marriage. "What's the special occasion?"

He strode into the room, his cowboy boots thudding softly on the brick floor. "It's our anniversary."

She straightened behind the desk, blinking fast. "Wedding anniversary?"

"Our fourth." He sat on the edge of the desk, his leg brushing her knee.

"Fourth," she said in a shaky voice. "Isn't it the husband who's supposed to forget?"

He knew her well enough to recognize she was attempting a joke to cover nerves. He wanted—needed—for her to be at ease, so he chuckled and teased her back. "You're off the hook for a gift, though."

He withdrew the present from inside his jacket, a flat box with a blue ribbon sporting sparkly horseshoes and the logo for the maker—Diamonds in the Rough.

She took the present tentatively, resting it on the desk in front of her. "You're so generous."

"I want you to be happy."

She tugged the bow carefully, slow in opening the gift as she always was on holidays. She lifted the lid to reveal a pounded pewter necklace with diamonds and a large teardrop Peruvian opal. Shana traced the details reverently. "This is lovely."

"It's a jeweler my mother and sisters use. Diamonds in the Rough is based out of Texas. They make unusual pieces."

"Thank you. This is really thoughtful. Again." Standing, she rested a hand over his and pressed her lips to his.

Her mouth was soft and familiar. The light touch of her tongue to his sent a bolt of desire spearing through him. The kiss wasn't over the top. Their bodies weren't even touching except for their mouths. But this woman had always turned him inside out in a way no other ever had. She held the kiss for another moment before easing back, her eyes blue flames.

He didn't push her for more. They had the whole night ahead of them. "I have a date planned to go with the necklace."

"A date, tonight?"

"Yes, an anniversary celebration. A first for you, and hopefully one worth remembering. Is there a problem?"

Her smile faded. "I have other plans, actually." She tapped the computer. "My work today paid off. A lead came through about the case."

"A lead?" He'd all but forgotten he'd asked her to do this. He certainly hadn't expected results so soon.

"Cross-referencing Milla Jones's emails and bank statements, there's a name that came up frequently, strangely so, given she hadn't lived here long."

"Interesting. Bank records?" He worked to keep his focus on her words, tough to do with the distracting scent of her teasing his every breath.

"Bank card transactions from him to her, shuffling money around. That can be iffy, of course, since shell corporations can make it too easy to hide who's really behind the money." She picked up a printout. "Anyway, I've got a lead that the guy's living at a local motel. If I can confirm that, I'll be able to trace more of his movements."

"Confirm it how?" Suddenly this job was starting to sound more complicated than he'd expected. He didn't want her digging into the backgrounds of people who might hold a grudge later.

"I'm going on a stakeout."

Alone? Like hell.

He shrugged out of his suit coat, more determined than ever to spend the evening with her. "Then I guess our anniversary plans have changed, because I'm going with you."

The decadence of this home—her home?—still caught Shana off guard sometimes. Even this closet was larger than her old apartment bedroom.

She stood in the threshold, gripping the door frame, her mind wandering back to her old cramped studio—the last place she actually remembered living. So different, with its exposed brick and water heater haphazardly placed next to the stove in her kitchen. A cheap countertop and a room with nonexistent closet space. She'd stuffed organized boxes under the bed for extra storage.

Now, before her, she took in a whole wall of shelves for shoes and sweaters, two walls with rows of clothes on hangers. And in the middle, a built-in island with drawers of jewelry and other accessories.

Her studio had been small, sure. But she knew its idiosyncrasies, knew everything in that tiny space followed rules of order because she had complete autonomy and authority. And yet, somewhere in the past five years, she'd learned to trust, to rely on another person. A man.

How had that transpired? Stress broiled in her stomach as she grasped for the truth. So she did what she'd often done as a young girl. She dialed her mom.

Shana clicked the phone onto Speaker as she stripped out of her oversize T-shirt and fluffy pajama pants. The cold air made her hair stand on end as she fidgeted with her plain white bra.

Opening the drawer of bras, she opted for a lacier number. Delicate and coy. Not that she planned on anything happening during a stakeout. But just for confidence's sake.

"Hey, Mom." Shana hooked the bra clasp, fingers moving for the Diamonds in the Rough necklace. The handcrafted piece laid flush against her breastbone, the cool metal somehow relaxing her.

"Hello, sweetheart. How are you feeling?"

Shana had told her mother about the pregnancy

right after the last doctor checkup. She just hadn't been able to keep the news to herself any longer.

"I feel great. Not at all nauseous. Appetite is well and I'm full of energy." In the center of the walk-in closet, a fat, off-white ottoman flanked a mirror. She sat, shoving her legs into dark-wash denim leggings.

"And your memory?" her mother asked with subdued but persistent urgency.

Shana buttoned her jeans, a long sigh heavy on her exhale. "Still nothing."

"I wish I could be there with you."

"I understand. Chuck's family is spoiling me. Chuck too." After pulling an oversize white sweater over her body, she moved to the mirror, adjusting the way it fell, fluffing her hair.

"I'm glad to hear you two are getting along."

The comment caught Shana off guard. She should have known better than to get too complacent.

She was almost scared to ask—and come to think of it, why hadn't she quizzed her mother more deeply on this? "Did Chuck and I have problems in our marriage?"

"You had arguments like any couple. He rushed through the romance so fast at first, I wasn't sure if I liked him. But with time, I could see he's a good man, and you two were very much in love."

Shana wanted to believe her mom, but would she have confided in her mother about marital problems? Maybe, but most likely not.

"Oh," her mother said, "happy anniversary."

And there was the answer to her question. It really was her anniversary. How paranoid to have thought he would make up something so easy to prove either way.

She really was overthinking things. She should just go on the stakeout with him and lose herself in the magnetism of her sexy husband.

When he'd made his anniversary plans, Chuck hadn't expected to end up going parking with his wife outside a seedy motel.

His five-star plans for the evening had been foiled by Shana's stakeout. No way in hell was he letting her do this alone.

Years in the boardroom had taught him how to improvise on the fly. He'd brought some of the luxury to her in his black SUV. Flipping on the seat heaters, he'd made the interior of the car as comfortable as possible while they did surveillance on the Snowdrop Inn—an old-school cheap motel with peeling paint and a weak light outside. Snow filtered down from the sky in a dusting on top of the snow-plowed piles. A moose ambled slowly through the parking lot.

Even without the flash of luxurious romance, the interior of his SUV seemed to have an ambience all its own tonight, jazz tunes playing softly from the radio. The casual dinner of burgers, fries and milkshakes had a first-date quality, a feeling he wanted to capitalize on even after they'd already finished their burgers. Chuck knew he had to win over his wife if he was going to get her back to his bed.

Despite the cold weather outside, the SUV hummed with promise. He'd provided the exact meal she craved, determined to pull out all the unconventional romance stops to make this work. And he couldn't deny that Shana was relaxed, happy, in her element.

God, she was mesmerizing in jeans, the new necklace he'd given her glittering against the simple white sweater. A camera rested in her lap, along with a small tablet. While this wasn't the evening he'd planned, he had high hopes it could still culminate in a satisfying end.

He draped his arm over the back of her seat, heat blasting through the vents. "How's the shake?"

"Amazing," she said blissfully, placing the cup back in the holder. "Funny how I never liked strawberry milkshakes or ice cream in the past and now I can't get enough."

He thought of prior pregnancies and how she'd craved berries then, too. But she wouldn't remember that, and he didn't see the need to bring up the heartbreak of those days.

"Glad you're enjoying it." He toyed with a strand of blond hair that had eased loose from her messy topknot. "I still want us to have a real anniversary celebration, though."

She angled her head to the side, smiling pensively. "Where did we go for our honeymoon?"

"We flew to Paris. We went to the Eiffel Tower and the Louvre." They'd been in love—or thought they were. Full of dreams for the future, no notion of how it could all implode under the stress of everyday life.

"Paris sounds romantic." She leaned her head back into his touch.

On purpose or by instinct? Either way, he was glad for the opportunity to be closer to her. He cupped her shoulder.

"We were there for two weeks. We only left our room twice to sightsee."

"Oh." Her eyes went wide, and her tongue touched her top lip, making him ache to kiss her.

Clearing his dry throat, he said, "We decided to come back another time for more sightseeing."

"Did we?" she asked, her voice breathy. "Go back, I mean."

"Yes, six months later." They'd had so much hope for the future then before real life hadn't turned out as blissfully as they'd expected. They'd had nowhere near the perfect marriage, nothing like his parents' union. "We planned to start trying for a baby soon and wanted to get traveling under our belt."

Except somehow most of those trips—other than on their first two anniversaries—were canceled at the last minute because of a crisis at the office, which led to more arguments about his workaholic ways.

She touched his chest lightly, bringing him back

to the present. "Where did we spend our first anniversary?"

"We went to Australia."

"That sounds incredible."

"It was." Sensual memories scrolled through his mind, making him ache from wanting her.

"Details?" she prodded.

He shot her a heated look, then said, "We went hiking, took a serious walkabout."

"Where are the photos? I would love to see them." She stirred the straw through the cup. "In fact, I can't believe I haven't asked to see more albums before now."

"Everything is on discs. I'll find them for you." Later. Delving too deeply into the past was dangerous territory.

"Thanks." Drinking her milkshake, she looked at him through her lashes. "I appreciate how open you are about discussing all of this, but I think it would be helpful to review parts of this on my own. Videos would be incredible."

"Duly noted," he said simply.

She set aside her shake and picked up her camera, snapping a photo of him. "So we never went to a cheap motel."

"This is a first. Should we check in?" he teased, half hoping she would say yes.

"I'm on the clock." She clicked more photos of him. "What about our second anniversary?"

"We went to a cabin and unplugged from the digital world." He tapped her arm to stop the photo session so he could see her eyes again.

"And our third?"

"For number three, we planned to go to Colorado, skiing."

"I know how to ski?" She laughed, smiling. "It sounds incredible. I wish I could remember."

The levity evaporated with the memory he wished he could forget. "We canceled our plans."

"Because?"

For once, his workaholic drive hadn't been the cause. "You had an early miscarriage. Neither of us felt much like partying." He scratched his chest over the tightness that never went away when he discussed that time, when it had really dawned on them that having a baby together might not happen for them.

Shana's hand slid over her stomach protectively. "Glenna said we discussed adoption."

"We did."

"Why didn't we follow through on that?"

He hesitated a beat too long, thinking about their rocky marriage over the past months. Would she notice his hesitation?

"Family issues with Mom's engagement put things on hold, then Jack was in a riding accident, then their wedding. There just wasn't a right time before you had the aneurysm."

"I hear your words—" she chewed her bottom lip "—but I also heard your silence."

"Nothing is ever clear-cut." Certainly not when it came to their relationship.

She tipped her head to the side, studying him through narrowed eyes. "Were we having marital troubles?"

That question posed a serious risk. He needed to be honest with her, but selectively so. If she found out they were separating, she could well bolt altogether—an unacceptable outcome.

"All marriages have bumps in the road. Fertility treatments took their toll. We'd decided to stop trying for a while."

"And that's everything?" Her forehead furrowed.

He needed to tread warily in case her memory returned. "It's difficult to share everything. We had arguments. No marriage is perfect." He scratched the back of his neck, weighing his words. "You have enough to deal with. How do I tell you about arguments without it sounding like I'm trying to excuse myself or without condemning myself?"

"Did you cheat on me?" she blurted out.

"No. Never," he said without hesitation.

No one compared to Shana. While their love had faded, the physical attraction had always burned intensely between them.

"I want to believe you." Her eyes were so earnest, blue flames in the glow of the dashboard light.

"I want that as well." He reached to stroke her cheek, his fingers sliding into her silky hair.

She swayed toward him, firing the barely banked

heat inside him back to life. The attraction between them was an undeniable constant. Four years ago at this time, they'd been finishing their wedding reception, anticipating being alone together on his private jet, starting their honeymoon.

Memories of that night stirred his desire higher. He urged her forward ever so carefully. Her hands flattened on his chest and he wondered for a moment if she intended to push him away. But then her fingers clenched in the flannel of his shirt and she pulled him forward.

Close. So close.

And then, yes. His mouth covered hers, her lips parting in welcome. Her hands slid up his chest and she looped her arms around his neck.

No hesitation. No doubt. She wanted this kiss, too. Wanted *him*.

Heat seared his veins, throbbing and gathering until he was hard from wanting her. Somehow, no matter what problems they faced, he could never get enough of this woman. Being inside her surpassed anything he'd felt before—and was all he could think about now.

His hand tunneled up beneath her sweater and he found the sweet curve of her breast encased in lace. She arched into his touch with a breathy sigh that caressed his cheek. Her head fell back and he pressed his lips to the vulnerable curve of her neck, right where he knew she liked best. He damn well would make the best use of his knowledge of what made her writhe with pleasure.

He needed every advantage he could get Shana.

He nipped her earlobe on the way back up to her lips—

Only to be stopped short as he caught sight of movement over her shoulder. A man and woman heading to the room Chuck and Shana had been watching all night.

The target had arrived.

Disappointment stung deep. As much as Chuck would have liked to ignore the world outside the SUV, he couldn't. They were here for a reason, an important one.

He would have to wait to finish that kiss—and to claim Shana as his once again.

Seven

Never before had Shana been disappointed that her job went well, but she couldn't deny she would have liked another moment to follow through on the attraction to Chuck.

But he'd given her this case, and she wanted to prove her independence, her business savvy. She owed it to him and to his family to help how she could.

A woman on a mission couldn't be stopped.

Shana pulled up her camera and started snapping photos. Better too many than not enough. She adjusted the lens, anchoring her focus on the man in the long, sleek black coat. Even in the dim lighting, she managed to capture a few images of his face.

She zoomed in more on his features, the weathered lines on his face. As for the woman, she seemed more guarded. For one, the woman had her back to them. Might this woman actually be Milla Jones? Could they be that lucky right away?

Maybe, it was certainly possible from the photos Shana had seen. The long blond hair and height were right.

Her pulse echoed in her ears with a jagged heartbeat, and her limbs sang with anticipation. She needed this to be right. Needed to prove something to herself. That she still had her sleuthing skills. That she could take revelatory photos and discern clues from the mundane breath of daily life.

And she'd be lying if she said she didn't want to impress her sexy, broad-shouldered husband.

Her fingers worked quickly, adjusting the camera as needed to obtain the clearest images.

She snapped a quick photo of the license plate, then shifted back to the couple.

He worked the key card, and Shana snagged additional photos of the man she suspected had sent the bank transactions. Time slipping by now. Shana trained her camera on the female suspect. Sending up a silent plea, Shana wished the woman would just glance over her shoulder. All she needed was a moment.

The female in question turned to get her overnight bag, the light shining on her face, a cigarette dangling out of the corner of her mouth, the tip glowing brighter in the night with a long drag.

There. The reveal.

Clicks like rapid fire, she captured the woman's face. Heart pounding. The thrill of her work coursing through her.

Chuck growled in frustration. "It's not Milla Jones."

"Are you sure?"

"Absolutely. About ten years older, and I never once saw Milla smoke."

Disappointment churned. It really would have been too simple for things to have worked out this quickly. Regardless, Shana had a lead on the guy, photos to track and his current vehicle.

"If you're certain, then I guess that's it for tonight."

Resting the camera in her lap, she snapped the lens cover back in place. As she moved, her fingers brushed against Chuck's jeans-clad leg. Butterflies took flight in her stomach.

Heat flared in his eyes. He ran a hand down the back of her neck. Subtle. Sexy as hell. "Sorry your stakeout was a bust."

Her neck still tingled from the casual touch. "Not a total bust. I got some photos and a license plate number. Those may still provide new leads. I just need to keep gathering the pieces." She drew in the last sip of her milkshake before tossing the cup in the trash sack. "So, what do you want to do for the rest of our anniversary?"

The question had sounded more innocent when she'd thought it. Now it filled the air between them, words loaded with a double meaning.

Her mind went back to the feel of his mouth on hers, his kiss, the familiar connection. It was a day to commemorate, and she desperately wanted to remember a part of that.

Which didn't seem to be happening.

After a night charged with tension, and romance all around them in the most unlikely of places, she craved some of that for herself.

"The question should be, what do you want, Shana?"

She licked her dry lips, unable to miss the way his eyes followed the movements. She looked at him through her lashes, then…hell, straight on. Direct. No coyness. "I want you to kiss me."

"I can definitely accommodate."

Hand cupping her chin, he breathed new life into her. The kiss was as intoxicating as wine to a parched palate.

The confines of the SUV proved tight. He guided her over the bucket seats onto the back bench, then climbed over to join her.

Like high schoolers on a date, they stretched out on the seat, him on top of her, kissing. And kissing. Luxuriating in the pleasure of connecting. Their bodies knew each other well, even though Shana's memory of their past had been wiped away.

He slid his hand under the hem of her sweater again, his palm to her back. She groaned with pleasure, grabbing his wrist and guiding it upward, higher and higher until he cupped her breast. One, then the other, he stroked until her nipples beaded in response.

Her hands were just as busy, curiously exploring his chest, down his back as she met him kiss for kiss, touch for touch.

His knee nestled between her legs, pressing against the core of her. She rolled her hips, husky sighs slipping between her lips as she worked against him.

"I want more than a kiss. I want you."

Chuck had driven home as fast as safely possible, his body on fire with the prospect of having his wife in his bed again.

Naked.

Under him.

Over him.

This wasn't an invitation he intended to turn down. Who would have thought a stakeout would be more of a turn-on than his plans of a dinner at a five-star restaurant with live music? His mind raced with plan B—places to make love to her...and the perfect solution came to mind.

Not in the bed.

But in the greenhouse.

Her favorite place on their property. Something damn special for this second chance to have Shana in his arms.

He steered the car past their home, the four-wheel drive managing the narrower path to the hothouse with no difficulty.

"Chuck, um, where are we going?" She glanced over at the barn as they passed by.

"I think every woman should be showered with flowers on her anniversary, and that's just what I intend for you. An abundance of them."

Already he could envision her wearing nothing but the necklace and flower petals in the warmth of the greenhouse.

Her gaze shifted forward as they approached the domed glass structure. Her mouth bowed in an "oh." He reveled in the pleased surprise on her face.

"I like the way you think, husband."

Husband.

That word seared through him. Her acknowledgment that she was his.

Hell yes, it was a primal thing. He couldn't deny it. Didn't want to.

She was his wife. Carrying his child. They were linked. The searing chemistry between them was their right to enjoy.

And he intended for them both to indulge to the max.

As they made their way from the SUV, he draped

an arm around her shoulders to keep her warm and make sure she didn't slip on the ice. Her curves fit against him in a way he remembered well and had missed lately.

He opened the greenhouse, a blast of humid warmth wafting out, carrying the floral perfume in the air. He drew her inside and swept the hood of her parka down, angling to seal his mouth to hers. She tasted of snowflakes and passion. Her hands gripped his jacket, urging him closer, but not nearly close enough.

With restless hands, he tugged off her parka and shucked his jacket, winter gear falling to the floor. With his hands bare, he stroked her back and lower, lifting her against him and deepening the kiss. Desire hummed through his veins, pulsing faster, harder. So much so, he considered setting her on the counter behind them and burying himself inside her now.

But that hadn't been his plan in coming here.

He eased back a step. She reached for him, and he kissed the tip of her nose. "Patience. I promise it will be worth the wait."

"I look forward to your delivering." Smiling, she leaned back against the wooden counter and watched him through sultry, narrowed eyes.

He strode to the reading nook in the back corner, an addition Shana had added for herself. Moonbeams streamed through the roof, illuminating the room along with the warm glow of heat lamps over seedlings. He pulled an afghan off the chaise and spread it on the floor, ever aware of her watchful gaze. Walking the length of the hothouse, he gathered irises and roses, plucking the petals and spreading them on the blanket. He turned to face her, his arms open.

She slipped off the counter and headed toward him without hesitation, her body a sultry glide of beauty that still left him breathless.

Sealing his mouth to hers again, he lost himself in the feel of her in his arms. Barely breaking contact, he peeled the sweater from her, sweeping it upward as she extended her arms to help him go all the faster.

"Shana," he said, eyeing her with reverence. "I want to take my time with you."

"That can absolutely happen, because we will be doing this more than once tonight." She tugged his belt loose. "Now let's get rid of these clothes so I can see you."

Her boldness surprised him, pleased him. He'd expected more hesitancy because of her amnesia. But he should have known. At the core, she was still his Shana. Bold. Unique. Ready to take what she wanted from the world.

At times he struggled with how that conflicted with her distrust of that same world, giving her a vulnerability he'd never quite grasped how to handle.

None of which he wanted to ponder right now with his beautiful wife shimmying out of her jeans in front of him.

He made haste to ditch his own clothes, his boots landing with a thud on top of her sweater. Until finally—*finally*—they were both bare. The appreciation in her eyes notched up his need for her as it dawned on him that—to her—this was their first time.

Slowly, carefully, he lowered her onto the afghan, the press of her body against the flower petals releasing a hint of perfume. He lifted a rose and trailed it along her skin, teasing whispers of pleasure from her lips. With each stroke of the rose, he traced the path with his mouth until her body writhed under his touch.

Her fingers gripped into his shoulders and she urged him upward over her, her legs parting to welcome him, her feet sliding up the backs of his calves. The warmth of her around him threatened to send him over the edge. It had been too long since they'd been together without a host of angry words placing a barrier between them.

Except he didn't want to think about the past now.

He just wanted to move, to thrust into his wife again and again, her hips arching up to meet him. Perspiration slicked their bodies, sealing flesh to flesh. Right now, he couldn't think of a better anniversary they'd shared.

His senses homed in to the here and now. The whoosh of the mister—the rustle of the leaves—the steam of the heated space—it was like a tropical haven in the middle of their storm-tossed landscape.

He rolled onto his back, and she purred her pleasure as she sat astride him. His fingers dug into the soft flesh of her hips, guiding her. Not that she seemed to need any assistance in knowing just how to move to drive him to the edge of completion. He gritted his teeth to hold back, determined to make this last as long as humanly possible—and to make sure she found her release.

Snow gathered on the clear glass roof, moonlight whispering through to cast honeyed beams along her creamy skin. Why had he never thought to do this with her here before? They'd made love countless times in the past, but there was a newness to this moment, to his wife.

His hands grazed upward to cup the sweet weight of her breasts, a perfect fit. He circled her nipples with his thumbs, teasing each into a hard bead of passion. All the while he watched her face, the way her eyes closed, how her nose flared with breathy sighs.

Then her spine arched and her head flung back. This, her body, he knew so well. She was close, and so was he. Restraint fell away and he guided her onto her back again, plunging inside her, savoring her husky cries of bliss that sent him plummeting into an explosion of sensation.

As aftershocks rippled through them, he grasped the edge of the blanket and draped the other half over them, petals whispering around them. He shifted, gathering her close to his side.

Shana rested her head on his chest. "Was it always like this between us?"

Such a complex question.

In some ways yes, but there had also been the tension of sex on a schedule to conceive, then the stress of their marriage crumbling. The attraction had always been intense, yet the pressures of life took away the abandon of living purely in the moment.

She tipped her head to look at him. "Did I say something wrong?"

Nothing slipped past her. Every misstep, pause, eye movement seemed to betray him.

"Not at all. Everything's right. And yes, we've always been this intensely attracted to each other."

That was true, at least.

"Hmm, I wish I could remember." Those alert, showstopping blue eyes fluttered shut, as if she was trying to conjure up the past.

A past he knew to be fraught with pain and complications.

A past he didn't want to burden her with now.

"Shhh." He kissed her temple. "Let's just enjoy the *now*."

So much easier said than done.

Stretching in her bed the next morning, Shana luxuriated in the flannel sheets against her well-loved flesh. Having sex with Chuck had been everything she'd imagined—and more. She couldn't imagine having forgotten a man like him, but she didn't intend to let regrets steal the pleasure of what they'd shared.

She vaguely remembered Chuck getting dressed in the greenhouse, then wrapping her in a blanket and carrying her to bed. He'd started to leave for the guest suite and she'd sleepily reached out a hand for him to stay.

And he did.

Beside her through the night, asleep still now.

She took the moment to study him at her leisure. He slept on his back, sprawling. He was a bed hog, and somehow knowing that intimate detail about him made her smile.

He was so in control in day-to-day life, the abandon during sleep touched her heart. He was such a strong man, but in sleep he seemed more…real. Less perfect. Which made him all the more endearing somehow.

More approachable?

An ease had settled between them during their lovemaking, as real and as corporeal as the light streaming through the oversize windows. Last night, she hadn't fought tooth and nail for a scrap of her past to come bounding back to her. Instead, she'd moved in the present.

Although last night, her body had certainly seemed to remember his well. She could still smell the sweet scent of flowers clinging to their bodies.

They'd certainly been in sync on a sensual level even if she had no recall of being with him before. Her flesh hummed with awareness of having been well loved.

The moment would have been perfect. Except she

kept remembering his hesitation when she'd asked if things had always been this way between them.

What was he keeping from her?

A pinprick.

That's what his hesitation felt like. Small, but deep. Capable of drawing both blood and infection. Shana believed him when he said he didn't cheat. That'd been her greatest fear, an unfortunate assumption that came from growing up with a wildly unfaithful father, a man who'd strung her mother along for years while he had a secret family on the side.

If not cheating, then what would cause the misstep? Something clearly made Chuck squirm in discomfort. Tapping her temple lightly, she again tried to will the knowledge.

And... Nothing.

Again, she felt like a spinning top, circling endlessly.

She wanted to believe in him, to have more nights like the one they'd just shared. There had to be something between them that she remembered on a subconscious level because she'd never been the sort to fall into bed with a man she barely knew.

Her fingers itched to stroke back the sweep of hair from across his forehead, but she feared waking him. She wanted to study him awhile longer as if gathering these minutes to herself could somehow make up for the deficit of losing five years. As if she could bring the balance to at least a hint more of equality.

So many questions piled up in her mind, and not

just about the time she was missing. Would their child look like him? What kind of parents would they make? Would she ever remember the night they'd made this child?

Her hand slid over her stomach, still flat. If it weren't for the ultrasound, she wouldn't have believed she was pregnant at all.

The amnesia had robbed her of so many things. But she wouldn't let it stop her from sleeping with him again.

She pressed her palm to the hard-muscled plane of his shoulders and stroked lower, lower still, until his eyes opened—groggy, sure, but a smile creased his face.

"Good morning, beautiful," he said, his voice early-morning hoarse.

"Good morning to you, too." She slung her leg over his, sliding closer just as—

The doorbell pealed through the house once, twice, then a voice called out, "Hello?"

Chuck's mother.

Again, his family was making themselves right at home. And their timing couldn't be any worse.

Eight

Yanking a thick cable-knit sweater over his head, Chuck charged down the stairs, toward his mother, who was still in the entryway. He didn't think she would actually come up to the second floor. Still, Jeannie and Shana had shared an ease and familiarity in the past. His wife had given his mom a key with Shana's blessing to use it.

But that was then.

Now things were so very different. His progress with Shana was hard-won. He couldn't take any risks that might upset the tenuous balance.

The heat of their night together was burned in his memory. Being with Shana had always been incredible, beyond anything he'd experienced with other women. But last night had surpassed even what had come before between them. He wanted to see where that connection could lead, but…

Jeannie leaned against the off-white couch. As always, his mother looked perfectly arranged. From the great window, sunlight glinted off her pearls. A staple of her wardrobe. Pearls that had been in the family for generations.

Moving farther into the living room, he feigned nonchalance as he pulled back the curtains. A light dusting of snow softened the horizon view, an elk leaving a trail of hoofprints on the pristine lawn.

"I'm sorry if I disrupted your morning," Jeannie apologized, nodding toward his bare feet. "I brought food—a simple chicken-and-rice dish that always settled my stomach when I was pregnant." She lifted a casserole dish, her smile genuine but concerned.

Growing up, food was what had woven together his family. Though lack of money had never plagued their family life, Jeannie refused to employ a cook. She'd preferred to prepare meals herself. Chuck's earliest memories always seemed to place him back in the grand Mikkelson kitchen and his mother moving between island countertop and stove, the scent of spices heavy in the air. She'd made sure they'd built traditions. They all ate in the kitchen, no formal dining room stuffiness. She made it clear to her children that values were more important than money.

Which made him itch now, thinking about how he was skirting the truth with Shana.

"Thanks, Mom. Luckily Shana hasn't been suffering from morning sickness yet, but we always welcome your cooking."

Taking the still-warm plate from his mother's manicured hands, he tilted his head, nodding toward the kitchen. A concerned smile still painted her lips as she smoothed her cream-colored cardigan before following him.

Toes touching the kitchen tile, Chuck tried to shake last night from his mind. He needed to focus on the present. He appreciated the support from his mother, but he ached to return to his bed, to Shana. He was anxious about the fragile rekindled connection. Hell, he wanted to bury his fingers in her honey-eyed hair.

Clearing her throat, his mother cut through Chuck's thoughts. "Will you be joining us at the rodeo tomorrow afternoon? We've got a ringside box to cheer on Marshall."

Chuck hadn't given it much thought, with his life in so much turmoil. But it sounded like a good possibility for a date night with Shana, while also further acclimating her to his new extended family.

Marshall Steele had run the rodeo circuit for years. He'd retired after a string of injuries. While he popped out of retirement on occasion, he now managed the Steele ranch about an hour away from their family mansion—which also sported a barn as big as some farms. The Steeles did nothing on a small scale.

Chuck took the glass casserole dish from his mother and opened the fridge. Tension knotted in his shoulders. In spite of trying to accommodate thoughts of family plans, memories of Shana and their hot night together fogged his mind.

Jeannie let out a little laugh, fidgeting around the room, strangely distracted. "It's not like you to sleep in."

"I took a couple of days off," he said carefully. His mom was intuitive when it came to her kids and he didn't want to risk her censure over him being selective in what he shared with Shana about their marital troubles. His mother didn't know about their plans to separate and he wanted to keep it that way.

"Like that ever made a difference to you before." She turned to face him again and took a seat. "You've always been an early bird."

Now he saw it in her eyes, the reason for her distractibility. She was concerned. As much as he wanted to rush her out the door and get back to Shana, he could spare a few moments to set her mind at ease.

Pulling a smile, Chuck nodded as his arm extended to the crisp white cabinets. His thumbs grazed the top of the glass as he pulled down a cut crystal tumbler. And then another. "Late night."

"That's right." She smiled knowingly. "Yesterday was your anniversary."

Opening the fridge again, he put space between her question and his answer, knowing how he responded would determine the remainder of the conversation. Snagging a bottle of sparkling water with a hint of lemon, he tilted the bottle to his mother in a silent question. And yeah, maybe he was stalling, too, because he felt guilty for not telling Shana the truth.

Jeannie's gracious smile brightened her face as she nodded yes. But it was clear she waited for a different kind of response.

Ah, now they were at the crux of why she'd shown up today. She was curious as well as concerned. "We went on a stakeout to follow a lead on Milla Jones."

Jeannie sat up straighter, her smile replaced by keen interest. "And?"

"It didn't work out." Well, the lead hadn't played out, but it had certainly borne fruit for him on a personal level. "I'll go wake Shana so you can visit."

"Don't bother her. Pregnant women sleep more."

Unscrewing the sparkling water's cap, he carefully poured the water before extending a glass to his mother. He knew that, about the extra sleep, but he didn't want to dwell on the painful past, or what might or might not be in their future, especially not after last night.

"I'm very excited about my next grandchild." She thumbed the band on her right hand, her ring from her first husband, who'd died. She wore Jack Steele's ring on her left hand now.

"Cautiously so, I hope. We've been down this road so many times and it didn't work out."

The pain of those losses stayed with him still. Although he intended to do everything in his power to keep his child safe. To keep Shana safe.

Except even a perfectionist like himself knew his best might not be enough.

"I'm happy today about the baby." She took his hands in hers and squeezed. "Joyful today. Let's enjoy the moment."

He picked through her words, searching for the takeaway. "Are you telling me I should stop worrying?"

"I wouldn't presume." She squeezed his hands again before letting go. "I know that's impossible given Shana's history with fertility issues, her amnesia and the pregnancy."

He sagged back to rest against the granite counter, the weight of concern tugging at him. And he couldn't deny the need to confide at least part of his worry to his mother. "If the doctor could give us a concrete reason why we keep having trouble... If there was something we could try that we hadn't already. It's not like bedrest would even make a difference. You probably aren't surprised to hear I have a problem with accepting things I can't change."

"We would give our own lives for our children. That's natural." She cupped his face with one hand and patted. "I'm here for you anytime, and I don't just mean with casseroles."

He realized that. His whole family was there for him. They were tight that way, and he felt guilty for not holding up his end of things lately. "I'm sorry not to be as present at work these days."

"Focus on what's important," she said without hesitation. "Everyone understands you've got a lot on your plate right now."

"You and Jack deserve to enjoy retirement—and being newlyweds." Saying that still felt strange. Blending families—especially large, powerful families like the Steeles and the Mikkelsons—had been tougher than expected, even taking into consideration the two families' business feud. Thinking about it gave him new insight into how painful Shana's life must have been after her father's betrayal.

"Don't worry about the office, son. We have plenty of children between us to share the workload. You'll end up owing someone something for helping you. Perhaps naming rights."

He hadn't even dared think about baby names. He and Shana had done that far too often only to be crushingly disappointed. But unloading those fears onto his mom might well open the floodgates to sharing others.

He'd built a careful house of cards here trying to win Shana back so they could have a life together and he wasn't risking it.

He didn't fail.

He settled on a lighthearted answer. "Letting the family pick names could go way wrong."

She rolled her eyes. "Especially if Aiden gets a say."

Which brought up a whole other concern. Chuck was too damn distractible these days, which was ironic since he spent most of his time working to distract Shana. Keeping her off the scent of his deception wasn't easy, but he needed to forge ahead with the only strategy he had to win back his wife.

"Are Aiden and Alayna still flirting with each other?"

"It's a crush," Jeannie said dismissively. "He's leaving for Juneau in the fall, transferring colleges."

"A lot can happen between now and then."

"Like I told Shana, they're both over eighteen—"

"Adults living under your roof."

"True enough." She nodded without conceding. But she meant well, and her love was unquestionable. "I know your life feels chaotic right now, and that can make a person search for other things to control. But trust me, son. Jack and I have got this."

There was nothing more he could do other than keep watch. His mother wasn't the only stubborn one. "Fair enough."

She eyed him for a few moments as if she might press him further. Then she sighed, picking up her sparkling water and sitting at the kitchen island. "Now tell me about the progress Shana's making looking for Milla Jones."

Chuck embraced the subject change, grateful for the distraction from talk of Shana. He needed time to get his head in order before facing his sexy, irresistible wife again.

* * *

Shana was scared to trust that all this joy could be real, holding Chuck's hand as he led her through the rodeo crowd to their private section of the enclosed arena. The warmth and familiarity of his grip sent tingles through her, stirring memories of making love.

She had an attentive husband with chemistry off the charts. They had a baby on the way. And he was doing his best to romance her whether they were on a date for dinner or a stakeout or with family at a rodeo.

A high-pitched whinny cut through the cold Alaskan air, echoing in her chest. Something about the sheer excitement of it all also knitted rough-hewn anticipation into her very bones. Even the wind whipping across her cheeks caught her off guard, making her wonder if she was, in fact, dreaming.

Chuck opened a wooden bar, waving her toward their section of bleachers, which was already packed with Steeles and Mikkelsons. A bombardment of greetings swirled around her just before she and Chuck were separated by Jack dragging Chuck into a discussion. Her husband dropped a kiss on her lips with a quick apology before joining his stepfather.

She didn't protest, and actually welcomed a bit of distance to regain her footing. Truth be told, the events of her life these past few weeks felt surreal. Hard to trust. Hard to believe, even though she moved through a seemingly perfect setup. The kind of life she'd never dared imagine to be hers.

Therein lay some of Shana's cellular-level hesitation, a sixth sense of something amiss sounding a dull, constant warning in her head.

She shook off the premonition and looked around her. She'd never attended a rodeo before. Everything she knew about them had been gleaned from television shows. The real-life experience was so much more intense. The scent of hay and leather. The loudspeaker piping country tunes, the whinny of horses echoing in the background. And people, so many people gathered in the arena, an audience decked out in different colors of boots, flannel and fringed shirts. Bright lights glistened off an array of the biggest buckles she'd ever seen.

Shifting in her seat, she couldn't deny how normal this felt. How natural. Catching a quick glimpse of Chuck, her stomach fluttered as she fully recognized the previously unnamed awareness. She could feel herself being drawn into this large family, the sort of family she'd dreamed of having while growing up as an only child with a distant father. Discovering her father had built that large family with another woman had been devastating to both Shana and her mom.

Again, she found her thoughts running to the past. But the distant past, not the past five years. Fidgeting in her seat, she picked at the ends of her hair. In some way, this repetitive motion grounded her to the present, to the sights and sounds of the here and now.

Though she sat beside Naomi, her eyes traced the muscular outline of Chuck's broad shoulders. She appreciated the hint of his back muscles in that tight gray shirt. The deep rumble of masculine laughter drew her eyes to his seat mates—Jack Steele and Jack Steele's much younger brother, Conrad. The trio appeared immersed in light conversation, judging by the way Conrad kept chuckling.

Her gaze fell away from the sights and sounds of her immediate vicinity and turned to her curiosity about the arena and the explosion of energy in the ring. A paint horse turned on a hairpin around one of the barrels. The young woman in a pink Stetson hat with silver embellishments seemed like a shooting star. Around the second barrel, the crowd gave an audible gasp as the rider lifted from her deep seat, nearly falling off the side.

Tension mounted in Shana's throat. Seconds felt like years. Somehow, the girl managed to recover, throwing herself back into the saddle. Silently, Shana hoped this girl would make the best time. She felt a kinship to that tenacity.

As the horse and rider effortlessly curled around the third barrel, Shana felt the anxiety in her shoulders release as she relaxed into the teeming box filled with both Mikkelson and Steele family members.

Jack, the patriarch of the Steele clan, held a beer bottle in his left hand as he laughed and chatted with other family members. Ice Cap Beer, the family brewery, was one of the corporate sponsors for the rodeo. Banners featuring a scenic glacial lake, the immediately recognizable Ice Cap Beer logo, lined the arena between other banner-sized advertisements for feed stores and Western wear.

Naomi let out a gentle sigh beside her, bobbing her head, that dark, signature ponytail revealing the sharp, beautiful angles of her face. One of the twins slept soundly in her arms, seemingly unbothered by the chaos.

Shana's hand slid over her stomach and she thought of her own child. This time next year, would she and Chuck be sitting here with their baby?

Chuck said there had been other pregnancies. She didn't remember them, but even contemplating the loss was difficult.

Shana swallowed deep, feeling her throat clog with bubbling emotions. Forcing herself to the present, she leaned over to Naomi, softly brushing the woman's shoulder in a cream sweater. "I can't believe the twins are sleeping through all of this noise."

Naomi smiled, her dark eyes dancing. "Any opportunity to wear them out, and the fact that they're both tired at the same time is nothing short of a miracle."

"They're beautiful." Shana skimmed her fingers lightly over the infant's feathery-soft dark hair.

"Thank you," Naomi said with unmistakable pride. "There are days I wonder how I'll make it until bedtime, but truly they are good babies. So far, it's doable to take them to the office with me, although I imagine that will change as soon as they're walking."

"I don't know how you juggle it all."

"Royce is amazing." Naomi beamed with love as she looked at her husband for a moment before turning her attention back to Shana. "I heard the stakeout was a bust."

As far as work, it was. Personally? It had netted pleasurable results.

"I haven't given up on that lead. It just didn't pan out this time. Surveillance operations require patience and persistence."

"I've always been in awe of your career. You're so daring."

Daring? The adjective disarmed her. How had she given up that part of her identity? Shana couldn't imagine not working. Giving up her job felt like an alien concept, like someone else's decision. But she didn't have the passage of time that had eased her into that decision.

"You're a legal eagle." Shana had dreamed of being a lawyer but there hadn't been the money to attend law school. "That's plenty impressive. And you manage it all while juggling twins."

"Shana, hon, you may not remember me, but I know you well. You'll manage the working mother routine with ease, if returning to your job again is the path you choose."

She hoped so. Life felt so overwhelming, so much

to process at once, like she was riding one of those bulls and had nothing familiar to hold on to.

A roar from the crowd cut her thoughts short as Marshall burst into the ring on the back of a bucking horse. The Steeles and Mikkelsons shot to their feet, whooping and whistling their support.

The vibration of her phone with an incoming message distracted her. The subject line kicked her heart rate up a notch. Familiar nodes of anticipation worked through her nervous system as she read.

A tip that Milla had been spotted coming and going from the hotel they'd staked out earlier.

Could this be another false lead? Or was this legit?

She should be focused on the job, and yet her first thought was elation over the possibility of a sexy repeat of her last stakeout with Chuck.

Alayna had been going to rodeos all her life.

Rodeos brimmed with heart-pounding moments, though Alayna had previously believed such moments were mostly reserved for the riders. But as she stood in her brand-new cowgirl boots, boot-cut jeans and a formfitting turquoise plaid shirt, she realized the fallibility of her previous assessment.

Because she was here with Aiden.

She couldn't have dreamed up being ringside with Aiden Steele, down by the chutes where all the action happened.

But here she was anyway.

Aiden had invited her to come with him to help

his older brother Marshall tack up his horse. Like the Steeles, she'd grown up around horses. But rodeo show life required a whole new set of rules, down to how the mane and tail were groomed and shined. Aiden had explained that the fancy polish that made the horse's coat gleam was part of the theatrics of the whole thing.

It wasn't enough to be good. Anyone could be good. Stars were made with these extra touches. Apparently, Marshall had been the best before injury forced him to take a slower pace.

Alayna toyed with a lock of her hair. "You know a lot about the rodeo circuit."

Aiden adjusted his black Stetson, looking like a natural part of this landscape in his worn jeans and flannel. "We supported my brother. I've been going to these since I was in elementary school."

"Did you ever think of trying your hand at it?" Just the thought of him in the arena in chaps sounded hot.

"Nah," he said, nudging his Stetson back. "It's my brother's gig. In a family as big as mine, it's tough to find a niche that hasn't already been mastered by someone else."

She understood about struggling to step out of the shadow of overachieving siblings. "That doesn't mean you couldn't be just as good, or even better."

"Easy for you to say." Aiden climbed on the second rung of the fence and leaned forward, looking wistfully at the current horse and rider. Exhaling hard, he hopped down. Leaning heavily against a beat-up barrel, he kicked dirt. "You're a straight-A student with a natural seat on a horse."

Heat rose in her cheeks, but she did her best to school her features into neutrality. The giddiness at his compliment still entered her voice, though. "You've watched me riding?"

He gave her that grin that sent her stomach turning barrel rolls. "We do live together."

"But we're not related," she reminded him, and herself. "Not really."

He snorted on a dry laugh. "Tell that to our parents. They're really over the top with the whole blended family thing."

"No kidding. I wish they would stop forcing the issue and just let us find our own pace." But no one had asked for her opinion. Apparently, since she didn't work for the corporation, she didn't count. "My mom's always been crazy big on family, though. She even put up with her sister giving her son away to us."

"I forget sometimes that Trystan isn't your biological brother, that he's actually your cousin."

"Aunt Willa and their brother—Uncle Lyle—had drug problems. Mom never gave up on them." Alayna stared out at a horse that flat-out refused to do anything but a working trot, despite the desperation on the rider's face. "I think if they showed up today, Mom would still throw them a banquet and start searching for rehab facilities."

"Is that such a bad thing?"

"If they're going to hurt my mom?" She shot upright, fired up. "Then yes, that's a bad thing. And our cousin—second cousin—Sage Hammond is related to them, too. She's been embarrassed and hurt enough by the grief they've brought on the family."

His eyebrows raised as he looked at her in surprise. "You're fiercer than I would have expected."

"Right, I'm the family mouse," she said with distaste.

"More like a kitten." He lifted her hands, his thumb stroking along her fingers. "With surprise claws."

His light caress sent shivers through her. She could hardly believe he was finally noticing her—touching her. "I'm glad you think so."

She was already anticipating the feel of his hands on her again.

"I'm leaving here, you know. I'm not sticking around home forever."

"Juneau isn't the end of the earth. We'll still see you."

"Um, it's not that simple."

She stepped closer, near enough to catch the scent of soap on him.

"Kitten, this isn't a good idea."

His words nicked her, reopening a wound. She leaned against the fence, eyes fixed on the next barrel racer. She did her best to seem normal and steady as she turned to look at him, letting her hair pool over her shoulder.

"What isn't a good idea?" she asked innocently. She wasn't giving up, but she sure wasn't going to look like an idiot, especially since they sat at the same dinner table every day.

A different kind of heart pounding took over her still-ragged chest. She turned away from Aiden, needing to collect herself, to look anywhere but at him. She scanned the crowd, trying to draw a full breath against the sting of disappointment.

Her eyes snagged on a face.

A face she remembered from somewhere.

Fear and adrenaline coursed through her as she forced air into her lungs. Had she really seen the profile of a person who had lied to her family?

There was no way to prove today that what she'd heard as a child was true. She wasn't even completely sure of what she'd heard.

She just knew there were faces that still gave her nightmares.

One face she could swear was, against all odds, right here in this arena, right now.

Fear had her digging her kitten claws into Aiden's steady arm. "You have to help me."

Chuck hadn't expected their rodeo date to end quite this way, but he had Shana alone and that was his top priority. They would end the night going to bed together. He needed to be patient.

She had received a tip that the man she was sur-
veilling would be back at the same seedy motel tonight, an odd pattern that did bear checking out.

And Chuck certainly didn't want her to be out
here alone. His sharp eyes followed the people that
passed by, entering and exiting the various rooms.

Shana shifted in the seat next to him, her camera
and tablet in her lap. "Are you sure you want to stay,
too? This isn't a risky stakeout and it could go late."

"I'm spending time with you." He stroked her hair,
testing the silky texture between his fingers. Even
as he remained patient—for the moment—he still
couldn't deny the need to move faster with winning
her over.

His mother's visit had reminded him too well that
anyone in his family could accidentally let something
slip around Shana that would blow up his world.

"Yes, I am exactly where I want to be," he said.

"You could work rather than simply watching
me."

He grinned. "I could."

"But you're not." She passed him her tablet.
"Here. I can make handwritten notes."

"No thank you." He passed the tablet back to her.
He wasn't taking his eyes off her or the motel until
he had her safely home. Then he intended to have his
hands all over her. "We've established I'm a workaholic."

She tipped her head to the side, her arms crossed
under her full breasts. "And I'm supposed to be-

lieve you've magically morphed into a footloose and fancy-free sort?"

God, he enjoyed her spunk. The urge to claim her, to move faster toward their reunion, nearly overwhelmed him.

"That would be overstating things. Let's say I'm working on delegating when appropriate." He lifted her hand. "And I know when it's time for recreation."

He pressed a kiss to the inside of her wrist, then angled up to her neck.

She sighed for an instant before easing away. "I'm a one-person shop. Delegating isn't an option. Now stop distracting me, you tempting man."

"I'm not going to argue with you."

A deep-throated laugh accompanied a pop of berries into her mouth. Her tongue teased his fingertips ever so slightly.

Damn. This woman drove him up a wall. Awareness ramping up, he did his best to draw his attention back to the movement outside.

An elderly couple hobbled by. Not them.

But from the corner, he spotted a woman with a blond ponytail. Could this be Ms. Milla Jones at last? He felt the urge to run out and see the woman up close. To know for certain. But they'd made the mistake of thinking it might be Milla before.

Shana reached for the door handle. "I can't get the angle I need with the camera."

He clasped her elbow. "You're not going alone."

She glanced over her shoulder. "Then be inconspicuous."

"I'll keep you close like any loving husband escorting his wife in for a tryst." He ducked outside into the light shower of snow, walking around the front of the SUV to her side. "Wife—"

He slid his arm around her shoulders, holding her close. Her curves pressed to him even through their parkas. He ached for this stakeout to bear fruit so they could—

No sooner had he finished the thought than the couple at the door seemed to catch sight of them. The pair took off, picking their way through the icy parking lot at a fast clip.

Chuck gripped Shana's shoulders. "I do not want you running on the ice. Period. It's too risky. I've got this."

She nodded tightly. "Go. Please."

As he took off, her words, "Be careful," carried on the snowy wind. Every footfall pushed him through the snow-covered lot, weaving between cars. He heard the chirp of a car door being unlocked remotely, lights flashing ahead. He made a beeline for the sedan, his boots gaining solid traction.

He reached the car just as the couple slid to a stop against the hood. The headlights illuminated their faces.

Their familiar, young faces.

Anger boiled to the surface, fast and furious.

"Aiden Steele, what the hell are you doing here with my sister?"

Nine

Shana bolted from the SUV at a sprint after Chuck.

She scrambled through the mix of snow and dirt that threatened to sidetrack her booted feet and upend her balance. Not fast enough for Chuck's rage, it seemed.

His anger was unmistakable and unsettling. If he charged up to the teens in this frame of mind, no good could come of the confrontation.

She remembered too many arguments between her parents. Her mother's suspicions, met with cold anger, then silence from Shana's father. Conflict still made Shana's chest go tight, but she couldn't back down from this.

Something about Alayna reminded her of herself at that age.

There'd been no one to intervene in Shana's life during those moments of vulnerability, though she certainly prayed for someone to come along. She'd wished on every evening star. But now, Shana could make a difference. A deep gulp of night air temporarily assuaged the thumping and squeezing sensation in her chest.

"Chuck," she called out. "Chuck, wait. Think about your frame of mind."

He didn't so much as glance back at her over his shoulder. He strode toward the young couple under the Snowdrop Inn sign, the last two *N*s flickering as the bulbs gasped their last breaths.

If Shana had been three steps faster, she could have caught up, but there was no stopping him.

Chuck's arm shot out and he grabbed Aiden by the back of his jacket. "What the hell do you think you're doing here with my sister?"

Alayna squeaked in surprise.

Aiden turned, his jaw jutting with defiance. "Trying to keep her out of trouble."

"You have a funny way of showing it." Chuck's tone was less a statement, more of an accusing bark.

Shana touched her husband's elbow, praying for restraint. "Careful, Chuck, he's a kid."

From across the parking lot, a beat-up SUV sputtered to life, cutting the stillness of the night. And somehow the lurching sound of the engine only heightened the bubbling tension between the Steele youth and the Mikkelson man.

For a moment, Shana averted her gaze, focused on the dull twinkle of the icicles on the roof of the Snowdrop Inn.

Aiden's shoulders braced in defiance. "I'm nineteen."

Great. Just what she needed. More testosterone in play. Shana held her calm. "Chuck, take a breath. Think."

Chuck's fist fell away from the teen's jacket. "Talk, boy. And don't try to BS me."

Alayna stepped between them. "Stop. I'm the one who wanted to come here." She held up a mittened hand. "Don't explode. We're not here for the reason you seem to think."

Chuck rocked back on his boots, easing off, for the moment at least. "Explain then, please."

Shana breathed a sigh of relief that they were talking, not fighting. She rubbed her arms to ward off a chill that had nothing to do with the icy wind.

"Let's move to the SUV to talk. It's crazy cold out here and there are people wandering in and out."

If Milla Jones was here and saw Chuck, that could be catastrophic. All the more reason to get back in the vehicle ASAP.

Chuck nodded tightly, bracing Shana's elbow as they walked along the slick lot on their way back to the vehicle. Cars slowly moved past, dim lights temporarily illuminating the blacktop path back to the dark SUV. Shana opened the door, reveling in the lingering warmth inside.

Once they were all in the vehicle, Chuck started the engine, cranked the heat and turned to the teens in the back seat. "Okay, I'm listening."

His sister chewed her chapped lip for a moment before launching in. "I saw someone at the arena that, well," Alayna rambled softly, "it's tough to explain. But someone I thought my imagination had made up. Seeing the person for real made me want to know for sure. Aiden didn't want me to follow all on my own."

Shana twisted to the side in her seat to get a better look at the nervous teens. Alayna tugged off her plaid scarf, toying with it. Shana could practically feel the girl's nerves.

"You're right," Chuck said drily, pulling off his Stetson and resting it on his knee. "It does make a strange sort of sense. It's so convoluted I actually believe you're telling the truth. Who did you think you saw?"

Alayna exchanged glances with Aiden before continuing, "Someone who left Alaska a long time ago and has no reason to come back." Dome light beaming overhead, Alayna's blue eyes shone with confusion and a hint of wariness. "And I haven't seen him in a long time, so I could be wrong. But it looked like Uncle Lyle."

"Uncle Lyle?" Shana asked.

Chuck shifted toward her. "Mom's loser brother.

His showing up would be surprising, sure. He hasn't been around in probably ten years or so. Alayna, why would you care?"

His sister hugged herself tighter, her body language shouting insecurity, as if she expected to be discounted. "Everyone's so worried about what that woman Milla Jones said, and I wanted to do my part to help."

Chuck sighed with exasperation. "What does that have to do with Uncle Lyle?"

"Um, well…" Alayna picked through the tassels on her scarf. "He disappeared not too long after that mysterious plane crash. It just seemed like Mom's brother and sister were always wanting things, like money. And they really wanted the Steeles to fail so Mom and Dad would be more successful."

The details sparked Shana's sleuth mind with possibilities. Having amnesia gave her an objectivity she might not have had before, since she was less attached to these people. How strange to have an upside to losing her memory.

Lyle was also related to one of the company's personal assistants—Sage Hammond. Shana made a mental note to look deeper into Sage's background and interview her about this Lyle character. She also needed to review the photos from the first stakeout.

Wouldn't Chuck have recognized his uncle? A lot of time had passed, though.

Chuck's mouth thinned before he continued, "I'm

still not making the connection as to why you and Aiden followed a Lyle look-alike to a seedy motel."

Headlights from a lone car washed the SUV in a sickly yellow light, illuminating Alayna's sheet-white face. She looked ghostlike in her puffed purple jacket. "I've always thought Uncle Lyle had something to do with that plane crash."

Shana held back a gasp of surprise. Clearly the girl believed what she was saying, but how?

"That's a pretty, um, substantial leap. You must have a reason."

"When I was a kid, I overheard a conversation between Uncle Lyle and some guy I didn't know. It didn't make sense then. I think I was too scared, too young, to trust what I heard. But over the years that conversation has haunted my dreams. Seeing his face tonight made me wonder if maybe..."

Chuck pinned Alayna with a laser-fierce gaze. "If you're right, then following him was the last thing you should have done. Do you realize you could have put your life at risk?"

Her brows knitted in clear frustration as a vein surfaced on her forehead. Then Alayna visibly deflated, her hands wringing her scarf tighter, knuckles blanched. "You still don't believe me."

"I believe that you believe it, and I believe you aren't trying to hook up with Aiden."

The boy nodded with a tight smile. "Thanks."

Alayna leaned forward to grip the seat in front of her. "So, are we going to check out the lead?"

"Shana is going to drive you both home," Chuck said with a voice that brooked no argument. "I'll drive Aiden's vehicle and follow."

Alayna's shoulders braced with ire, unusual from the normally passive girl. "You have no right."

Shana rested her hand on Chuck's arm. "How about you and I just follow Aiden and Alayna to make sure they're home safe and sound?"

Muscles flexed under her touch but finally Chuck nodded. "That's acceptable."

Acceptable? Shana couldn't help but wonder who this stern man was, so different from the tender lover who showered her with ice cream and flowers.

A chilling reminder that she really didn't know him at all.

The drive to the Steele home had been strained, to say the least, but then, Chuck didn't feel much like chitchat.

His sister's strange words and erratic behavior had rattled him. That his uncle could somehow be involved with the plane crash that had killed Jack Steele's wife and daughter seemed a stretch. Uncle Lyle wasn't sharp, by a long shot. He couldn't have pulled off something of that magnitude—or that horrible.

Alayna must be wrong.

Chuck prayed she was wrong.

He shook free of those thoughts and focused on

following the car ahead of him as Aiden pulled up to the rustic Steele mansion on the water.

Chuck glanced over at his silent wife in the passenger seat. Something wasn't right with Shana, but he couldn't deal with that just yet. He had another crisis at hand to settle first.

Sliding into the Steele driveway, he threw the SUV into Park so quickly, the automobile seemed to stutter and exhale a sigh that echoed his own.

He needed to get to the bottom of this situation with Alayna. A belly-deep frustration moved through his blood. The cold Alaskan night grew more and more complicated.

Of course, he couldn't deny some of his focus on his sister had to do with trying to control something in his life.

Right now, he had to focus on making sure Aiden and Alayna were safely home and not running rogue with stakeouts of their own.

Some answers about what Alayna thought she'd heard would be helpful, too.

As silent as an encroaching shadow, he followed the two teens up the stairs to the house. Absently, he held the door for Shana, whose normally bright face sported knitted brows and chapped lips in a neutral line.

The group moved into the great room, a fire crackling and popping in the massive fireplace. Their party wasn't exactly loud. In fact, no one had spoken for some time. Still, the shuffling of bodies into the living room caused Jack and Jeannie to look up from their overstuffed leather sofa.

Chuck's mother and his new stepfather had been curled up on the sofa, enjoying the evening in front of the fire, if the wineglasses and cheese spread on the coffee table were any indication.

It was strange for him still, Chuck admitted, to see them like this. For his family to now include once mortal business enemies. A blended family had its challenges, for sure, but the Steele-Mikkelson merger felt fraught with even more than potential corporate espionage and possibly murderous consequences, according to the slanderous statements made by Milla Jones.

And, if Alayna's half-formed childhood memory was to be believed, Uncle Lyle's statements, as well.

And that's what Chuck needed to focus on, not how differently he'd hoped this evening would end for him and Shana.

Jack and Jeannie were clearly startled by their entry. Chuck couldn't blame them. He hadn't called or texted. He'd simply acted on instinct, knowing he needed to be here. To talk in person. To sort out this mess. Perhaps Jack and Jeannie would have insights into Alayna's strange memories.

Chuck was less and less sure that asking Shana to take on this case was a good idea.

Jeannie touched her chest in surprise. "Chuck, Shana, what a surprise. What brings you two here tonight?"

Jack was as imposing as the antlers mounted above the fireplace. Broad and tough as nails, Jack cocked his head to the side. Though his stature had always been imposing, the Steele patriarch was gentle in the way he put an arm around his new wife.

Chuck didn't begrudge his mother her happiness, but it felt strange to surrender control of his family to this man because of some whirlwind romance that had flipped everyone's world upside down.

Chuck ran a hand down the back of his neck, about to drop a helluva story. "Shana and I were on a stakeout after the rodeo and we found these two—" he pointed to Aiden and Alayna, standing warily to the side "—going into a motel together."

Shana moved protectively toward his sister.

Jeannie gasped.

Jack scowled.

Not a good start, but there was no easy way into this, for too many reasons.

Alayna grabbed her mother's arm. "We explained it to them already. I saw Uncle Lyle at the rodeo—"

Jeannie discarded the plaid blanket that had draped around her shoulders. "He lives down in Montana."

"Well, I thought I saw him—" Alayna sounded less certain now "—and it made me remember things, especially with all of this talk about Milla Jones. Uncle Lyle wanted to hurt the Steeles, and we're all a family now."

Neither Jack nor Jeannie looked much like they

believed her. Still, the older Steele stepped up. "You should have come straight to us."

"You're looking at me like I'm crazy," Alayna cried. "I wanted proof and I had Aiden with me."

Jack glared at his youngest son. "*You* should have spoken to us."

"She was moving fast," Aiden protested lamely.

Jack glared. "You have a phone."

Aiden shrugged without meeting their eyes.

Chuck's radar went on alert again as he wondered if there was something going on between Aiden and Alayna, an attraction at the very least, which would make it all the tougher to weed through Alayna's strange behavior and supposed memories.

Memories.

A beast all the way around these days—what had been forgotten by Shana, what had been remembered by his sister. Although he was more certain than ever that his sister's recollections were faulty, the product of muddled nightmares from a tough time in their past mixing with a stressful present.

And a need to get time alone with a certain Steele teen.

Jeannie squeezed her son's arm. "Thank you for taking care of this and bringing them home. Jack and I will handle it from here."

Chuck stalled. That was it?

He was supposed to back down about Alayna and Aiden sneaking around together? He'd been in charge of the family since his father's death and now his mother was making it clear his help was no longer needed?

His family's old mortal enemy was now the de facto dad.

When the hell had the world turned so crazy?

Chuck felt the sting of his mom's dismissal, deeply. Although maybe it was just as well that he step aside, since he needed to focus on Shana, for tonight and for their future.

Then he caught the scowl on his wife's face and stopped short, remembering she wasn't the least bit happy with him anymore.

As confused as ever when it came to Shana, he sensed he was running out of time.

The echoing silence from Chuck sent Shana burrowing deep into her mind, hurt on Alayna's behalf at how Chuck had handled things tonight.

She thought about saying something to him…but then she realized the tension she'd felt from him in the car came from a different source than she'd first thought.

Chuck was radiating pain.

She'd been so focused on herself, she hadn't fully considered all he'd been through with her health scare, the miscarriages, his father dying, his mother remarrying. He'd been so attentive to her every whim—without asking for anything in return.

Perhaps the time had come to quit fighting the flow and just see where life led them. After the tense evening, Shana was more than ready to lose herself in their heated connection, so she could only imagine how he was feeling. Rather than an impulsive night of intimacy, she wanted to invite him back into their bedroom to stay while they worked through her lack of memories.

"Chuck, do you think we could put aside what happened with your sister for now? There's nothing more we can accomplish tonight."

His hands clenched around the steering wheel. "It has been a long day. You should probably rest."

She stroked a hand along his arm. "I'm not in the least tired. Are you?"

He looked at her quickly, his eyebrows lifting in surprise. Then fire lit his expression. He stroked back her hair and cupped her face. "Sleep is the last thing on my mind."

"I'm glad we're on the same page about how to spend the rest of the night."

Her fingertips quivered in anticipation, her mind filling with the promise of deep kisses and twining bodies. Chuck navigated the car into the garage, careful to avoid the other vehicles lined up in the large bay.

Mind set, she reached for her door handle, anticipation singing through her veins.

With lightning speed, Chuck moved out of the car, and positioned himself by the door to the house before Shana had a boot-covered foot on the cool pavement. He gave her a sheepish smile as he opened the side entrance to their home.

As she shimmied out of her parka, her skin reveled at the warmth of the house. After placing her jacket on a hook, she shook out her hair, feeling freer and more comfortable than she had in weeks, confident in her choice, in her desire for him. Yanking off her boots, she smiled to herself, ready for this.

Crouching, he lined up their boots on the racks along the floor of the large coatroom. "You handled things well with my sister. I shouldn't have lost my temper."

She felt the heat of his gaze as he looked up at her. Those emerald green eyes seared her to her core, making her feel aware and awake. Shana's breath hitched for a moment.

Fire danced between them.

He offered her a hand. With soft footfalls, he started down the side hallway to the back staircase. Alight with a new kind of intense desire for this man, her husband, she kept pace alongside him.

"I get that you're worried about your sister." She stroked his arm. "That's understandable. I'm just sorry I haven't unearthed more information about Milla Jones."

They climbed the stairs, moving through the hallway where Alaskan landscapes hung on the wall, mixed with family and couple photos in muted gold frames.

An image of them in hiking gear in Australia tugged at her.

The photo also reminded her of how painful this time must be for him, having his wife forget about him. This should be a gloriously happy time in their marriage, expecting a child. Instead, she was floundering her way through her feelings for him, not to mention getting to know his entire family.

"I don't expect magic from the investigation, Shana. Every piece to the puzzle will eventually get us there." He stopped outside the master suite, leaning against the door frame, his eyes distant.

"Like putting together my memory." Five years of memories with this man—her husband, the father of her child—just gone. "I wish I remembered our past."

She stroked his face, tears and longing clogging her throat.

He cupped her hand and pressed it closer to his skin. "I have the honor of making you fall in love with me all over again."

His words made her heart flip inside her chest.

She couldn't claim to be in love with him, but she understood they must have been in love before. With his devotion to recapturing that again, how could she help but be moved?

One thing was without question.

Their chemistry was off the charts.

And while she couldn't seem to reclaim the memories she'd lost, she was determined to fill the present with fresh ones.

She arched up to skim her lips against his. "Come back to our bedroom. Make love to me."

With a low, sexy growl of consent, he sealed his mouth to hers. He reached behind her to open the bedroom door. Chuck scooped her into his arms and carried her across the threshold into her bedroom.

Their bedroom.

It felt so natural, so right, to be in his strong arms. Yes, she understood that he had an advantage because he knew her body so well. But instinct seemed to lead her just as surely; she knew just how to touch him, too.

Slowly, he eased her to her feet again, sliding her down the length of his body while sprinkling kisses along her face, her neck, nipping her earlobe. Hunger grew, flaring. Their hands swept away clothes, perfectly synchronized in brushing aside all barriers between them.

The backs of her bare legs bumped the bed, and he lowered her onto the broad expanse, never taking his eyes off her. His eyes flaming with desire, he knelt beside her, the mattress shifting with his weight.

Side by side they lay, his caresses intense and reverent all at once. He was so different from the angry, overprotective brother from earlier. Back to the man she'd come to know.

The husband determined to romance her.

And she was quite happy to be wooed by his seductive caresses. To forget her concerns and grasp hope, to hold her husband.

To lose herself in long, passionate kisses.

Her restless legs kicked aside the downy comforter. Her foot glided along his calf as she met him touch for touch, stroke for stroke. She savored the feel of his hard muscled body, honed from years outdoors. He wasn't just a man behind a desk. And he wasn't a cowboy in name only.

He was all man, earthy and sexy.

And hers.

He hooked an arm behind her knee and inched her leg higher, bringing her closer until…yes…the steely heat of him pressed against her core.

His eyes met hers, as he held her, as he slowly, ever so deliberately, slid inside her.

The delicious warmth of his thickness filled her with his warmth and with a sense of how right this was. Her body knew him, remembered him in a way that her mind still wrestled to rediscover.

Awash in sensation, she surrendered to the elemental. To pleasure rippling along her every nerve. She combed her hands into his wayward hair and drew him closer for another taste, tongues meeting and mating in a thrust and caress that matched their bodies.

Bliss built, taking her higher, faster, but she didn't even consider holding back because there would be more. She would have him in her bed for many nights to come, giving her time to explore every incredible inch of him at her leisure.

The power of her release gripped her in wave after

wave of ecstasy. She arched into each pulsing tremor rocking through her. Chuck's hoarse shouts mingled with her sighs as they found their climax together.

She hadn't thought anything could top their time together in the greenhouse, but there had been something special to this moment, with its promise of more.

Sweat cooling on her body, she languished in his arms, melting in the aftermath. Her fingers drew lazy circles down her husband's strong arm, along the defined muscles.

Chuck pulled the downy comforter over her and kissed her forehead. "I'll go get us some food. The rodeo refreshments feels like forever ago."

"Don't they, though?"

So much had happened in one evening, which likely explained her exhaustion. Or maybe pregnancy symptoms were finally catching up with her. She'd been following the doctor's orders to the letter, keeping in mind past miscarriages. She touched her stomach, thinking about the baby growing there.

It seemed surreal. Chuck's child.

Rolling to her back, she flung her arm overhead, stretching before swinging her feet to the floor. She tugged on Chuck's T-shirt, breathing in the scent of him, his voice drifting from the hall and over her senses.

A call? This late?

Curiosity piqued, she padded across the room. He

had his cell on speakerphone, his voice a low rumble, his words indistinguishable. And the other voice…

A woman.

Shana resisted the urge to step closer to the door and listen. It was probably just a family member or a work call. There was no reason to be suspicious.

Other than the fact that she remembered nothing about their marriage.

Her head started aching, her mind filled with other memories, of her father and how her mother hadn't suspected his deception—right up to the point when she was confronted by the other woman.

Shana pressed her fingertips to her throbbing forehead. She needed to stop her roiling thoughts before she worked herself into a total meltdown. She needed to de-stress. Maybe a shower would help. At least it would keep her from standing here eavesdropping.

She made fast tracks to the bathroom and turned on the shower jets. Peeling off the T-shirt, she squeezed her eyes shut against the headache, willing it to go away. She stepped into the steamy stall, jets hitting her from all sides and easing her tense muscles.

Still, her mind spun, and she pressed her palm against the tile wall.

Flashes of memories blazed through her mind, like bursts of electricity.

Standing at the altar with Chuck.

Their anniversary trips became real, parts of them at least.

Overwhelmed, she sagged back, her legs unsteady.

The reel of fragmented memories culminated in an image of her throwing his clothes angrily into his suitcase, of her demanding that they separate.

She heard herself asking him for a divorce.

Oh God.

She pressed her fist to her mouth to hold back a cry.

How could Chuck have kept this from her? How could he have pretended this whole time?

Because she was pregnant.

The obvious answer.

She doubled over, grief and agony wracking through her. Tears streamed down her face, mixing with the pelting water. She didn't need to remember more. She didn't want to.

This was too much. It threatened to tear her in two. The pain was so intense it felt more than emotional.

It felt...

Real.

Her stomach cramped harder, harder still. Her knees gave way as she realized.

She was losing the baby.

Ten

Heart slugging in his chest, fear shredding his gut, Chuck paced in the ER waiting area.

He considered calling his family, but just couldn't find the will to say the words out loud, words that would further end what had been a period of hope for him and for Shana.

Her panicked voice still echoed in his ears. He'd hung up on his call from work and raced to her, finding her tugging on a robe while doubled over in pain.

He hadn't needed her to tell him what was happening. They'd been through this before.

The pain. The loss. The grief.

She'd been silent for the whole drive, not that he had felt much like talking, either. Fear for her seared him, threatening his focus as he guided the SUV along the icy roads. An ambulance would have taken longer, and he couldn't bring himself to think about losing her, too.

The door to her exam room opened. His stomach lurched. The nurse gave him a sympathetic smile and waved him through. "You can see her now, Mr. Mikkelson."

Shana lay on the examination table, her face as pale as the sheet covering her. "I lost the baby."

Her voice was flat, beaten down, weary, and somehow her tone was more upsetting than outright tears.

Tears, he could handle and wipe away.

Right now, he didn't have a clue what to do for her, and that made him feel helpless as hell.

"I know. I'm so sorry."

"You don't have to try and make me feel better." Her fingers clutched the sheet, twisting it in her tight fists. "I know you're hurting over this, too."

He sank down into a chair, each drag of air stinging him with the antiseptic smell of defeat. "I knew the odds were against us. If there was anything in modern medicine left to try, we would have tried it. There isn't."

He needed to box up his own hurt over the loss, the pain no easier this time than it had been the first. If anything, it devastated him more. But somehow, he knew Shana hurt even worse.

She felt the loss even more deeply for having been the one to carry the child inside her.

"The doctor said much the same," she said in that flat voice, refusing to meet his eyes, "that we couldn't have done anything differently."

"Shana." He reached for her hand.

She pulled away. "You don't have to."

Why wasn't she looking at him?

He couldn't shake the feeling that something else was going on with her. "What do you mean?"

She shifted against the pillow, sitting up with a wince, her gaze skating to him briefly, then flicking past. "After we…uh…when I was in the shower, some of my memory returned."

Chuck swallowed hard.

The worst-case scenario ran through his head like a warning siren. From her closed-off pose, it seemed she hadn't recalled their wedding and honeymoon, but something far darker.

"What part?"

Her eyes met his solidly for the first time, and he saw more than hurt staining the blue depths. Outright anger flared.

"The part where we decided to separate."

Words froze in his throat, in his mind. He'd entertained the notion of her remembering, but he had hoped she would recall happier times.

Anything but this.

"I don't know what to say."

"Nothing. There's nothing you can say now," she

retorted tightly, swaying. "The time to tell me the truth has passed."

He steadied her, gripping her shoulders. His first priority needed to be keeping her as calm as possible. "I didn't want to upset you. We can discuss this later."

"Later?" She shrugged away his touch. "There's nothing more to talk about. Ever. I realize now that you were staying with me out of a sense of duty, because I was pregnant. But I'm not now. You can go."

Like hell.

"I'm not leaving you."

"The doctor said I need to stay here overnight. But you don't have to stay."

"I'm not leaving," he repeated.

Blue fire sparked in her eyes, and her normally upturned lips thinned into an uncompromising line. "You have no obligation to me anymore."

He understood she had to be upset—about what she'd remembered, about what he hadn't said—but this complete slicing away was a surprise.

"This isn't the time to make big decisions. You're emotional." He paused, scrubbing a hand over his jaw. "As am I, truth be told."

Her brows shot skyward. That gorgeous face tightened with anger. "We've already had this discussion. There's no more talking to be done. I'm sorry. But it's time for us to end things."

End things.

The second time their marriage had been declared over.

He searched for words to…what?

To not have this cold silence between them.

The ER door opened, admitting two staff members ready to move her to a room for the night.

Shana reclined back. "Chuck, you should go now. Please."

The slight crack in her voice kept him from arguing with her. But no way was he leaving the building.

He'd told himself he was staying with her because he couldn't let their marriage fail, especially not when they had been expecting a baby, but now he found himself thinking of all they'd shared since her amnesia.

And he couldn't just forget about that, not like she seemed determined to do.

Chuck didn't know what the future held for them. But for tonight? He was staying close to his wife.

After a restless night in an uncomfortable hospital bed with disquieting dreams startling her awake, Shana was no closer to repairing her broken heart.

How could she have become so attached so quickly to the idea of a future with Chuck when she barely knew him? She ached for everything she had lost and what could have been.

But whatever they would have created, it would have all been built on lies.

The hospital door opened, and Shana steeled

herself for the possible impact of Chuck walking through.

Except it wasn't him. And it wasn't a nurse.

"Mom," Shana said, her voice wobbling.

Her mother strode across the room and wrapped Shana in a familiar hug. Her mother smelled of lilac and orange blossom, her signature scent. Though it hadn't always been. After finding out about her husband's secret family, Shana's mother had somersaulted, understandably. But the day she regained her footing was the same day she'd started wearing this scent.

For her mom, lilacs and orange blossoms marked hope, new beginnings.

The now-familiar fragrance comforted Shana as she looked at her elegantly styled mother, whose steel-gray hair flowed down her back in a sleek ponytail. Her mother had put her life together again with poise, grit and determination.

Her mom had always been there for Shana growing up, and she'd only moved on after...

The memory flickered, like a snowy mist Shana could barely push through, the frigid haze stinging. Her mom had moved forward with her dating life once Shana became engaged to Chuck. He'd proposed on a dinner cruise along the Alaska coast on a magnificent night with a sky full of northern lights.

Her throat clogged with tears.

She swallowed hard and said, "Mom, why are you here? How did you arrive so quickly?"

Her mother eased back. "Chuck called me last night and told me about the baby. He's worried about you. I caught a red-eye flight."

"But your vacation days—"

"Don't worry about me." Her mother smoothed back Shana's hair. "I'm here for you. I would have come sooner but I thought it was best for you and Chuck to... I thought maybe..." She shook her head. "Never mind. Let's focus on the present."

"Thank you for coming. You must be exhausted after the night flight."

The smile lines by her mother's gray eyes deepened. Squeezing Shana's hand as if to dismiss her concern, she continued, "We can rest once we get you home."

"I'm going to be fine."

Her heart was shattered but her body would recover.

For a moment, her mother's slender face—normally sunny and full of life—seemed blanched of color. She focused those storm-gray eyes on Shana, a sad smile dusting her lips. "I've been through what you're experiencing."

Shana looked up in surprise. "You miscarried? You never told me. I mean, you didn't tell me when I was growing up. Maybe you did in the past five years and I don't remember."

She'd only recovered a small portion of her memories. And she sure didn't like some of what she'd seen. Fresh hurt cramped her belly for all her losses.

"I did share when it first happened to you." Her mother sighed sadly, pressing a hand to her chest, smoothing along the collar of her orange sweater. "When you were a child, there just didn't seem to be a time or reason. Then when you were a teen, there was…so much else going on."

So much else with her father.

The wreckage of his actions had left a wake of grief and distrust that still tainted their lives. His choices had effectively made a lie of anything seemingly positive he'd done in the past, because it had all been covered in a cloak of deception.

Shana pressed her hand to her heart. How could Chuck have lied to her, too, knowing how much the truth meant to her?

She blinked back tears, wary of letting her emotions rise to the surface now. She might lose control completely. She just wanted to get home, to bed.

Except her home was Chuck's home.

Theirs together.

A shaky exhale rocked her. She had few choices for now. She needed to recover first.

"Well, Mom, I guess it's no surprise my brain defaulted to amnesia." Bitterness stung her tongue. "Our family has been good at keeping secrets."

"Or trying to put a positive spin on everything as if that covers the pain." Her mother nervously picked at her chipped polish.

"Thoughts that are too deep for me today, I'm afraid."

"Of course. Let me help you get dressed to check out of the hospital. Chuck is at the nurses' station getting the discharge paperwork rolling."

He was still here?

"Chuck? I told him he could go."

Her mother's beautiful face scrunched in surprise. "Why would you do that?"

Chuck hadn't told her mother about the separation. And he hadn't left.

She should have known he wouldn't listen. He'd given in too easily last night. That same sense of duty and obligation that had made him stay with her after her memory loss was making him stick around now.

But having him nearby hurt too much. She would accept the ride home to keep the peace, but after that they needed to talk about how to sever ties for good.

The next day had brought no peace, but Chuck took some comfort in action, accomplishing things by rote, restoring some form of order to his chaotic world.

By the time the doctor had cleared Shana, the paperwork had been completed and they'd driven home, dark had already set in due to the shortening days in Alaska now that winter approached. But there would be no holiday celebrations together for them this year, or any other.

He believed her when she said they were over. She remembered enough, and his deception now had sealed the deal.

He'd rolled the dice and lost.

Back home, Chuck settled his mother-in-law in her suite with a light dinner, although he imagined she would be asleep on her way to the pillow. Shana had gone straight to their room without a word. Not that he suffered any delusions that he was welcome back in the bed beside her, to comfort her the way he'd done in the past.

But she needed to eat. And he wasn't going to take no for an answer.

He carried a tray of food—pesto meatballs made of lean moose alongside skewers of mozzarella, grape tomatoes and spinach. Hot tea finished out the meal, steaming the scent of spices into the air.

Shana sat on the small white sofa by the fireplace. Moonlight splayed over the mountain scape, downward and through the window. Her blond hair glowed with a honey hue that made him ache to haul her into his lap and press her head to his chest. Her pale paisley robe made him think of watching her reach for it when stepping out of a shared shower.

They'd worked so damn hard to save their marriage, to have a child, and all of that had burned away, like ashes in the grate.

He set the tray on the claw-footed coffee table in front of her. "You need to eat."

She glanced at him, her eyes shadowed. "Thank you for the food, and for calling my mother."

"I'm glad Louise is here for you." He'd held back on contacting his family, not wanting Shana to be exhausted by a flood of people. Well-meaning people, but a mass, all the same. He didn't want her to feel overwhelmed. "Can I get you anything else?"

"No thank you." Her voice was hoarse with held-back tears.

"Shana," he said, his gut clenching. "For what it's worth, I'm so damn sorry."

She studied his face for five heavy heartbeats before saying wearily, "I wish I could believe things would be different between us. But it's so hard to trust anyone after what my father did to my mother."

Unsure how much she remembered now, he let her continue, curious to see where this conversation would lead, if it could bring either of them peace.

She shook her head, clutching the neck of her robe closed. "Never mind. I'm sure we've talked about this before."

"You don't remember those conversations between us?" he prodded, sitting in a chair on the other side of the fireplace, the flames crackling in the early evening quiet. "Maybe it will help jog more memories if you talk."

"It seems silly to repeat it when I know you know."

He didn't answer.

"Fine," she caved. "I'm not going to go through all the gory details, though. I've thought it through so many different ways and why I can't seem to get over it. Unless, maybe I did get over it while we were married?" She watched him out of the corner of her eyes as she filled a plate with dinner.

"I'm sorry he hurt you so deeply." He meant it. Wished he had more to offer her than words. "We both have our fair share of baggage."

"What's yours? Other than lying."

He winced. He couldn't deny what he'd done, and it stung like hell because he considered himself a man of impeccable honor, professionally and personally. He realized now what a mistake he'd made, but he'd been so desperate to accept the second chance for his marriage.

"I'm a perfectionist and a workaholic." He picked up a plate, not really feeling much like eating but wanting to encourage her to do so. She needed to regain her strength. "I expected too much from both of us and our marriage."

"And I kept miscarrying." Her hand went to her stomach.

"I never thought that." He took her dish from her and held her hand. "Wipe that notion out of your mind."

"I want to."

"Then trust me on this much at least." He willed her to believe him, not that willing it had ever worked in the past. "Okay? Now, please, I want to hear what you're thinking about your dad."

"All right… My father liked to give gifts. When he was on the road—which was a lot—he would send elaborate presents for missed birthdays and holidays. I pretended to like them, but I just wanted him home."

"That had to be difficult when you found out the truth of where he'd been during those absences."

"Understatement." Her blue eyes took on a far-away look. "He kept sending things afterward, too, as if nothing had changed. I think that's what both-ered me most. He really expected us to pretend life was the same…that what he had done was some-how normal or justified. I threw each gift away un-opened."

He leaned forward, setting aside his untouched plate. "You never told me that before." What would have happened if he'd been patient about listening before rather than just growing angry over her lack of trust? "I'm sorry if my gifts were triggers for you."

"You're always thoughtful in what you give. It's not some generic present… Not that I know if my fa-ther ever got better at his choices." She toyed with the spear of cheese and veggies. "I should have donated the presents to charity. It was wasteful to trash them." She popped a mozzarella square into her mouth.

He noticed she still hadn't denied his gift giving had been counterproductive. *Meaning well* wasn't good enough. Gifts weren't a substitute for heart-felt actions.

"You have nothing to apologize for."

"I get too wrapped up in my own pain, past and present. I know that."

He'd always considered her to be strong, so much so he didn't always know what he had to offer her. "You have reasons to grieve. We both do. You lost your father. We've lost children...and we've lost our marriage."

She set down her plate, looking as disinterested in food as he felt. "I wish I remembered more."

"No, you shouldn't."

"That bad, was it?" A tear slid down her cheek.

"Parts," he said honestly. He clenched his fists to keep from reaching for her, knowing she would push him away as she'd done in the past.

"Okay then." She stared at him bleakly. "Where do we go from here?"

"If you're going to leave me, I just ask that we wait to tell everyone until after the big shareholders' gala next week." Not that he gave a damn about any celebration, but he wanted an excuse to keep her here to recover before they finalized any decisions. "Can you promise me that, for my family?"

She nodded wearily. "Until then."

Two words.

Just two words that signified the second and final end of their marriage.

Eleven

The week passed too quickly for Shana to process the shift in her life. Flashes of memories kept knocking her off-balance just when she thought she'd found a hint of stable ground.

Sitting in her spacious dressing room with her mother and Alayna, Shana struggled to hold back tears. Makeup and cosmetic brushes spread out in front of her, she prepped for the steampunk-themed ball, sweeping shadow on for a smoky eye effect. She blended the warm brown tone on the outer corner of her eye, letting the soft brush bristles distract her from the messier aspects of the forthcoming night. Patting a shimmery gold into her inner eye corner, she took a deep breath, debating which shade of red lipstick would best complement her saloon-girl-inspired gown. She adjusted the straps on her dress, her hair piled on top of her head in a mass of curls.

The past week had been…hell.

Staying with Chuck while the end of their marriage ticked away was like inflicting paper cuts on her already raw emotions. Having her mother on hand had offered a buffer of sorts by keeping things from imploding into a horrible argument.

Not that Chuck showed any signs of temper. He seemed to be just counting down the clock until they could both officially call things quits between them.

Their only interaction all week had been about the investigation. She'd traced the man photographed at the hotel and it wasn't the infamous Uncle Lyle.

They'd also looked into Sage Hammond, all done with computer searches in bed while Shana rested and recovered. It had been difficult to imagine Sage might be involved. The woman was a shy relative, much like Alayna. A solid worker for the company. For all appearances, she seemed to be loyal, with an unblemished record.

There was no more work to accomplish on that front. No more days left to maintain the facade of a happy marriage for the family's business reputation.

Pretending at the gala tonight would be yet another, deeper level of hell.

At least Chuck's family had stayed away for the most part, respecting Chuck's request for space. Unusual in his big family. She remembered that much from her slowly returning memories. His relatives were a caring lot, but a bit overwhelming. She didn't know how so many of the Steeles—and now Mikkelsons, too—managed to live under the same roof, even with individual apartment-style suites of their own.

Apparently, the close quarters grated on Alayna, too, as she had shown up on Shana's doorstep tonight. The teen's makeup brushes were spread on the marble countertop, too. Shana's soon-to-be ex-sister-in-law swept bold neutrals onto her eyelids. Things had blown up at the Steele home when the teens were confronted by their parents. The argument had resulted in Aiden threatening to quit college and go work in the oil fields.

Heartbroken, Alayna had raced over to Shana's. At least the teen had already been dressed for the big gala so once she calmed down, she could still attend.

Any family member's absence would be conspicuous and a sign of dissention among the ranks.

Not good.

And for that reason, Shana was attending, even though her heart was shattered, too.

Alayna was rocking leather pants and spike-heeled boots with a cream-colored bustier, mining gear hung from her belt. The shy mouse was roaring for the steampunk gala.

Shana's mother, Louise, smiled brightly, costumed like a Victorian matron with a saucy little pillbox hat perched on top of her upswept steel-gray hair. She took over helping the teen with her makeup while Shana finished her own.

"There's no hurry to fall in love, sweetie."

Alayna rolled her eyes. "You're supposed to say that."

"If you feel that way, perhaps there's something to what I'm saying." Louise swirled a plump brush in a bright shade of fuchsia before tapping off the excess.

"I'm in love. I knew the moment I saw him."

Shana chased feathery memories of the first time she'd seen Chuck. He'd come to her office to subcontract out some security work. She'd fallen hard and fast for the sexy mogul with a rugged edge. Their wedding had been a fairy tale, her mom helping her with makeup then like tonight.

So many memories.

And no doubt so many more that would filter through and break her heart all over again.

Louise dabbed blush on Alayna's cheeks. "That's attraction. Love grows over time."

"How much time?" Alayna asked desperately, testing lipstick shades on the back of her wrist.

Shana's mother sighed, placing a hand on Alayna's shoulder, her pearl ring gleaming in the light. "There's no magic formula. But it takes time to learn about each other and to learn if you're compatible for the long haul."

Shana outlined her lips in a dusty red, satisfied with the edgier look that reflected her mood. "It takes time to figure out if someone's a smooth talker or genuine."

She'd thought Chuck was genuine. And in many ways, he had been. Memories of their time together this past week collided in her mind, reminding her how good they could be together.

Alayna dabbed her finger in sticky sequins and patted a line along one eyebrow, then the other. "And if the person's genuine, then it's love at first sight after all."

"What do your mother and Jack say?" Louise pressed wisely.

"They just keep freaking out. They're so into us being stepbrother and stepsister they seem to forget that Broderick and Glenna are married. It's like their romance doesn't count since it started before this whole big, weird family merger."

Shana adjusted her peacock feather and gear-inspired wrap bracelet. "You should be talking to your mom, Alayna."

"You can keep saying that, but it's not so easy. Everyone thinks she's, like, some kind of saint." Alayna looked up at Louise standing beside her. "Our family has secrets. You should meet Mom's sister. She actually abandoned her own son—Trystan—and let my mom and dad adopt him."

Shana put a hand on Alayna's arm. "Maybe we should table this discussion for now."

"I'm tired of how nobody talks about things. Don't you want to know all the things you've forgotten?"

One part of Shana wanted that more than air. Another part winced at the thought of any more heartache.

"That can be tricky since every person who tells me something has their own interpretation of what happened. I need to get a stronger sense of who I am now before I let people start coloring in the blank slate of the past five years." She leaned forward. "I think that's what my mother was getting at, when she said you were too young to be sure of love at first sight."

"Are you saying I'm a blank slate? Because I think that would be a little offensive." Alayna scrunched her nose.

"I'm saying you may not fully know yourself yet. You don't have as much perspective as people like our mothers. Give it time."

Yet even as Shana offered the advice, she knew the answers weren't always so simple. Especially since time had run out for her and Chuck. All she had left was a chance for one last dance with her husband, one final chance to be Mrs. Mikkelson before she said goodbye.

Savoring the new-wave folk tunes, Alayna swayed from side to side, each movement sinking her deeper into her spike-heeled boots.

The band was dressed in eclectic Victorian garb. The piano resembled a saloon upright. Alayna lost herself in the music pouring from the speaker—an oversize gramophone.

Her gaze picked its way across the room, working overtime to spot Aiden in the midst of Western memorabilia and technological gadgetry. She did her best to casually squint past the giant leathery hot air balloon in the center of the room. The open basket on the ground sported a flurry of cocktail tables with saloon girls and their pocket-watch-wearing dates.

Attempting to feign interest only in the impressive details of the ball, she let her gaze go up to the balloon's full height, admiring the twinkling lights arranged to look like faux fire.

Imagination wandering, Alayna pictured what it'd be like for Aiden to grab her hand, whisk her past that hot air balloon and to the dance floor, past steel-framed lightbulbs staggered and hanging from the ceiling connected by rust-kissed chains. A manufactured night sky of possibility that Alayna wanted to entertain. Big-time.

While not as cumbersome as finding him in a masquerade ball, the job of locating Aiden among the hat wear that made fascinators seem as boring as ball caps was proving difficult.

Normally, she would enjoy a party like this. The music, the historical riff—it sure beat the stuffy formal balls her family usually dragged her to. Her mom's assistant, Sage Hammond, had outdone herself with this edgy celebration for the Alaska Oil Barons, Inc., shareholders and board of directors.

If only Alayna and Aiden could be in the middle of the dance floor, partying...

She wanted to take the advice given to her, but it was hard being okay with the fact that Aiden was leaving, and not to a place she could follow him, like a college transfer to Juneau.

Everything was changing.

The lump in her throat threatened to return. Shoving those thoughts aside, she redoubled her search, moving through the crowd of coattails and wigs of piled curls.

"For the next few songs, we'd like to welcome to the stage Miss Ada Joy Powers," the lead singer of the band called into the microphone.

Alayna stopped on her heels, turning back to see the famous vocalist burst from behind the massive clock that featured oversize wheels and hands. Dry ice spewed fake fog as the noted soprano emerged, looking as mysterious as all get-out.

The crowd went wild.

"Thank you, thank you all," she said in a husky voice before nodding to the band to begin. "'It doesn't matter unless you give your heart to the moment. To the night...'" Ada Joy belted an original song into the microphone, bopping her hips from side to side in a tight bodice and saloon-girl-style skirt.

Just beside the stage, Alayna saw her cousin Sage. Her heart twinged as she saw Sage in a too-baggy schoolmarm dress. Sage appeared to be like part of the set, fading into the background. But she was the one responsible for overseeing every last detail of this evening.

Then finally, Alayna spotted Aiden—looking hot as always, rocking his costume. He wore a military-style jacket with leather knee boots and a bowler hat with pushed-up goggles.

Her heart pounded as she caught his dark, shining eyes. That signature wide smile spread across his face. He set down his drink on a nearby cocktail table and made strides towards her. His gaze lit as he took in her costume.

She savored this moment of him seeing her—really seeing her.

Alayna perched a hand on her hip as he stopped in front of her. "I can't believe you're really leaving college."

"I plan to go back, once I've had some time to find my way and learn the business from the ground up. I finally feel like I'm stepping out of my brothers' shadows."

She swallowed down tears. He looked so happy. And she wanted that for him.

"Be careful out there."

The oil fields could be dangerous. She'd grown up hearing about the accidents, and it chilled her to think of him putting himself at risk.

"*You* be careful chasing after crazy relatives. No going after them by yourself. Okay?"

She flipped her curled hair over her shoulder. "Sure."

"I'm not joking around. There are people who care about you who would be glad to help."

"Just not you," she couldn't resist saying.

He rested a hand on her shoulder and squeezed gently, his touch warm and tingly. "I gotta find a different path from my brothers. Different from my dad. I want to build my own future."

She wanted to lean into his hand, to see if he would pull her close.

Not that she believed he would. Especially not here.

"You know you're making me like you more."

His eyes roved up and down her once more and he smiled slowly. "You're going to be just fine, Alayna."

"Says the guy who told me to find bodyguards in my family."

He winked. "That's not what I meant."

"I know." And she did. If only he meant it enough to stick around. But he didn't. "Thanks."

He extended a hand. "Wanna dance?"

It wasn't everything she wanted. But she sure as hell wasn't going to turn him down. It would have to be enough.

For now.

Chuck pushed past the vintage locomotive at the entrance of the gala, ignoring the smile of the tuxedoed engineer with striped coattails and tall leather boots passing the party gifts to passersby who hadn't received one yet. The gifts, his cousin Sage had said a few weeks ago, would be brass pocket watches with the new Alaska Oil Barons, Inc., logo plus today's date.

He'd be damned if he wanted any additional mementos to mark the complete failure of his marriage.

He wanted to drink, to lose himself.

He couldn't take his eyes off Shana in that saloon girl costume, high in the front showcasing her killer legs, the back of the dress trailing longer. Her hair was piled up in a messy mass of curls that called to his hands to set them free.

Even from here, he could see her swaying to the music. She seemed to fit perfectly into the alternative history theme, the copper piping framing the thick-paned circular window behind the band a natural complement to her costume. He watched her maneuver through the crowd, toward the scaled-back nineteenth-century oil rig spewing deep red wine. And then he lost her in a sea of curls and goggle-adorned top hats.

He snagged a beer from a passing waiter dressed as a mechanic and moved toward Marshall. The middle Steele brother leaned against the high cocktail table. A plate sporting a picked-at chocolate top hat and mini savory meat pies was pushed against the vintage clock centerpiece.

Marshall brought his water glass—a vintage Mason jar—back to his lips, annoyance painting his face. He had one arm in a cast and sling, the result of a nasty horse accident last week at the close of the rodeo.

Chuck stood across from Marshall at the small cocktail table. "You don't look like you're having much fun. Can I get you a beer?"

"Nah, I'm good with this." Marshall lifted his water glass, lemon wedges mixed with ice, then gestured to the space around him. "Getting dressed up for a party isn't my gig. If I don't hold strong, the next thing I know the family will be hiring some image consultant to give me a makeover like they did to your poor brother."

Chuck laughed softly, his eyes skating to his brother, Trystan, happily dancing with that same image consultant who was just showing signs of pregnancy.

A fresh wave of pain, of loss, stabbed through him.

He shifted his focus back to Marshall before his gaze went searching for Shana for the hundredth time that night. No doubt she was still standing with her mom, his wife looking so damn beautiful it hurt.

"You're wearing what you wore to the rodeo last week."

The night Chuck's marriage had ended for good.

"Exactly," Marshall retorted. "I don't like costumes."

So he'd worn rodeo gear.

Chuck had to chuckle. "Wish I had thought of it."

He'd chosen black leather, a mix of miner and biker.

They both took swigs of their drinks. Marshall lowered his glass, his expression going somber. "Hey, I'm really sorry to hear about your wife's miscarriage."

"Thank you." Chuck couldn't say anything more. The loss had hit him hard. There was no getting used to grief. But losing Shana too made the pain cut even deeper.

Marshall's father, Jack, sporting a long black duster and a top hat, moved across the room, heading straight for their table.

"Chuck, how're you holding up?"

How was he supposed to answer that? "Shana's recovered."

A flat, stark answer. Sure. But there was nothing else he could hope to say.

Jack looked like he was going to press further, but then he simply clapped Chuck on the back. "Glad you're here. Nice costume."

Marshall swirled his glass until the ice clinked, looking sidelong at his father. "Is that a dig at me, Dad?"

"We're just happy you're here, son. That was quite a tumble you took at the end of the rodeo."

"Putting my horse away." He shook his head. "I feel like a damn idiot."

"We all make mistakes. It's called being human. You'll be saddled up again before you know it."

If only life was that simple.

Make a mistake. Saddle up again.

Marshall looked into his empty glass. "I'll go see about some refills for us. Be right back."

Chuck started to leave, too—he needed to schmooze with the guests—but he just couldn't scrounge much of a party spirit in spite of the country and western tunes being belted out by Miss Powers.

"Chuck? Something on your mind?" Jack waited, and when Chuck didn't answer, he continued, "I'm not trying to pry, and even though I'm married to your mother, I don't consider myself some kind of father figure to you. You had a great one. But we are family now, and it's clear something's weighing on you."

Chuck considered blowing off the discussion, but it wouldn't do any good. "Everyone will know soon enough. Shana's starting to recover her memory, including the problems we had. She's decided to leave me."

Jack's face tightened, his dark blue eyes wild like an Alaskan blizzard. "I'm sorry to hear that."

A bark of laughter fueled by regret escaped Chuck. "What? No advice on how I should fight for my marriage?"

"Best as I can tell, you both fought to save it for a while." Jack stroked his chin.

"We did."

"What's changed?"

He'd worked too much, demanded perfection of himself…of their marriage.

But all of that was old news.

"She doesn't trust me."

"Well, you did lie to her—a lie by hedging, but still, not telling her how bad things had been between the two of you maybe wasn't the right way to go."

Had their problems been that obvious to others even though they hadn't announced their separation?

Apparently they had.

"This little talk isn't making me feel much better."

Jack Steele turned to face Chuck, shoulders square, looking every bit as powerful and commanding as a king. "Do you want me to soft-soap things or do you want to keep your wife?"

Put that simply, the answer was obvious. "I want to keep my wife."

Jack shrugged. "Sounds like you have some groveling to do."

Chuck's eyes lingered on Shana, taking in the attentive way she listened to the couple chatting with her. She had a way of making people feel valued as she took in their every word. It made her a great detective—and a wonderful person.

"That simple?"

"If you mean it. Say it, live it, walk the walk and earn her trust back. Marriage isn't easy and it sure as hell isn't perfect. Call me an old romantic, but you two have a lot of love between you."

Love.

Hearing the word from the gruff Steele patriarch brought things into focus.

Hell yes, he loved his wife. Always had.

She'd loved him, too. Even when they were separating, she'd cried over how much she still loved him even as they couldn't see their way through.

He regretted lying to her to keep her.

He regretted a whole lot of things.

But had he told her how much? Had he ever really committed to being the kind of man she needed?

The answer shamed him. Especially when he could see things from her viewpoint now.

He recognized now how he'd never made a full-scale commitment to compromise. He'd spent the past two years devoted to filling his father's shoes. Sure, Chuck had taken time off and scaled back a few meetings periodically to appease Shana, but he hadn't made a legitimate effort to change his workaholic ways.

To be there for her.

He'd chosen unbridled ambition over his wife.

Was it any wonder she didn't trust in his love for her?

Now he stood at a crossroads.

Make a real change or lose his wife forever. And looked at so succinctly, the decision was the easiest of his life.

He wanted his wife back at any cost.

Shana had spent most of the party trying to break free of people so she could corner Chuck. She knew it shouldn't make any difference if she bided her time until after the gala to say goodbye, but the pain of waiting was just too much to bear.

She needed to speak with him.

Parked by an oversize metal globe near a food table, Shana struggled to steady her pulse, anticipation mounting in her chest as she again searched for her broad-shouldered husband.

Standing on her tiptoes, she looked over the heads dressed in Victorian garb, past goblets of wine held by the who's who of Alaska. She peered over the saloon girl in front of her, looking past the miniature top hat made of clock cogs and feathers. The live music had ended for now, a deejay taking over between sets.

Any other time, Shana might have struck up conversations with the people around her. But her body and soul hummed with urgency.

She needed to see Chuck.

Except every time she located him, by the time she made it across the crowded venue, he was out of sight once again. The event was a packed, unbridled success. And she couldn't find the will to celebrate anything.

She just wanted her husband.

Finally surrendering to waiting, she stepped out into the night air, flipping up the hood on her red velvet cape. She picked her way across the night to the steam locomotive positioned out front. Music echoed softly from the large hall. Flashes went off periodically as partiers took photos by the train car. She stuffed her gloved hands into her sleeves and perched on the train car's platform, her breath puffing clouds into the night air. Each cleansing breath should have ordered her thoughts, but the stakes were so high and she wasn't sure she had any more answers now than the times they'd failed before.

Just when she was ready to give up and go home, her eyes lit on the unmistakable form of her husband. His broad shoulders filled out the leather duster, his black Stetson catching snow on the brim.

"Chuck…" His name came out on a whisper.

One he must have somehow heard.

He turned toward her, his eyes lasering to her from across the walkway. He strode closer, as if he'd been looking for her, which couldn't be true, but still her heart leaped at the possibility.

Each step nearer made her heart speed in her chest as she searched for the right words to begin.

Grabbing hold of the railing, Chuck swung up onto the platform in a smooth, athletic move. Before she could speak, he locked an arm around her, pulling her flush against him. His eyes met hers. Words dried up in her throat, because she *knew* he was about to…

Kiss her.

His mouth slanted over hers, gently, teasing and tasting, giving her every opportunity to pull back if she wished. But the only thing she wanted right now was more of him.

Her hands clenched in the lapels of his coat, the heat of him searing her through the cape.

He swept her hair back from her face. "I know it's too soon for more," he said hoarsely. "I just wanted you to know how special you are to me. Would you step inside so we can talk?"

Why would she deny him when she wanted that very thing and his words made her heart light with a wary hope?

"I would like that."

It had been a long, sad week of distance between them. She couldn't imagine a lifetime of that.

Inside, the train compartment was finished in plush royal blues with gold fixtures. He gestured for her to sit on the lengthy sofa and took her hand in his, kneeling.

"I owe you an apology."

She listened, curious.

He squeezed her fingertips lightly. "I should have been honest with you when you first lost your memory. I didn't earn your trust, and just as bad, I didn't trust you."

"I did ask you for a divorce."

Even the partial memory of that day filled her with pain.

"And I didn't listen to what you needed now or then." He looked down at the floor for three thudding heartbeats before continuing, "I thought having a baby would somehow magically turn us into a family. But even just the two of us, together, we are—we should have always been—a family."

His words helped ease the grief of the other miscarriages she was starting to remember. She didn't know if she wanted to try again, not yet, but she knew for certain she didn't want children with any other man.

"Keep talking." Hope fanned higher, warmer.

"I was very lucky to have an easy childhood. I didn't fully realize how much of a mark your father's betrayal had left on you. I should have, and for that I'm so very sorry. Sorrier than I can say."

Surprise whispered through her, soothing old hurts. "Thank you—"

"I'm still not done. I love you, Shana Mikkelson." His words rang with conviction. "I love you more than any job, more than anyone else, more than life. And if you'll let me, I want to spend the rest of our days being a family, with you."

She peeled off her gloves and cupped his face in her hands. "Oh, Chuck, I love you, too, and I'm so sorry for the pain I caused you. We should have been comforting each other—you tried to comfort me— and I lashed out. I pushed you away at a time when your heart was hurting."

"You don't need to apologize to me."

"I do. I'm as much a part of this breakup as you are."

His forehead furrowed. "Did the rest of your memories return?"

"Not everything. But I remember the day we were married and other happy times, the way we felt. It's how I feel about you now. We have a love and marriage worth fighting for."

His eyes closed, and a heavy sigh of relief visibly wracked through him. "I'm so damn glad to hear you say that."

"I should have believed in you. It's clear to me now that you're a good man." She angled forward, resting her forehead against his. "We had love before. We didn't have trust. Now we have both. And I want to be your wife. Not just in name from my previous life, but now. Forever."

She nudged forward, knocking him back until they both stretched on the train car sofa. Kissing him as fully as he'd kissed her.

He palmed her waist, staring up at her, his heart in his eyes. "I'm happy and relieved to hear that because I love you so damn much. I can't imagine my life without you."

She had to know. "What if we never have children?"

"Then we don't. I can face anything as long I have you by my side." He kissed her slowly, reverently before saying, "I have ideas for our future and I want to hear yours, ways that we can make a new start."

A smile rose from her heart to her face. "I look forward to hearing them."

"Let's go home."
Home.
Here in his arms, she was already there.

Epilogue

One month later

Chuck pulled the satin coverlet over him and his wife, the railcar swaying ever so slightly as the train ate up the miles along the Canadian countryside.

He and Shana had enjoyed many romantic trips in their marriage, but this topped them all. Of course, trains would always hold a special place in his heart after they had found their way back to each other at the steampunk gala a month ago.

A lot had happened in the past few weeks as they worked to make good on their promises to build a new life together. Chuck's decision to back away from working long hours had been met by similar announcements from other Steele and Mikkelson siblings. Broderick and Glenna were expecting a baby. Trystan wasn't interested in taking more on his plate, in spite of his makeover. He wanted to focus on his family.

Marshall had made it damn clear he wasn't stepping into the void, even though he'd agreed to host a fund-raiser. He was chomping at the bit to get rid of his cast so he could resume ranching duties.

So the search had begun outside the families for a CEO for the Alaska Oil Barons, Inc.

Chuck had proposed a job change for himself. He would soon assume duties overseeing the pipeline operations on the North Dakota end—an offer accepted by the board of directors even though it was a step down for him. He and Shana had chosen this mode of land travel for a romantic getaway on their trip to house hunt for the impending move. While the North Dakota office didn't come with as much prestige or as many divisions to manage, he found himself excited for the change.

They were both revaluating their priorities these days.

And focusing on their marriage topped the list.

Relocating would also give them more privacy. No question, Chuck loved his family. But as a whole, they could be overwhelming. There would still be visits, and a corporate jet afforded the easy option of attending important family functions.

But they would have their own home, their own space.

"I can hardly believe you're making this change for me," Shana murmured, nuzzling his neck.

"For us."

"I'll never get tired of hearing that."

"Good to know." He slipped his hand around to the small of her back, her skin like silk. "How about this? I love everything about you and look forward to telling you every day."

"Hmm..." She sighed, sliding her bare leg between his. "And I love you and the life we're building together."

She was resuming her work part-time, having accepted a job in North Dakota to freelance for an established private detective agency once she moved. She wanted to keep her professional skills up to date, while also having time to travel. She was still looking into Milla Jones's disappearance and investigating the pasts of Jeannie Steele's siblings.

Shana and Chuck were both adjusting, perhaps in a way they should have before.

But they were also lucky.

They'd been given a second chance—by each other—and they were both committed to making the most of it.

Shana was remembering the past, slowly. Chuck was filling in the blanks for her as she asked. No holds barred. Some of the discussions were tough, but that also assured her of his honesty.

They didn't shy away from anything anymore.

They were building a future on a firm foundation.

Shana traced small circles on his shoulder, her wedding rings glinting, the set complete on her finger again. "This trip has been idyllic. I've been thinking we should do this more often."

"What do you have in mind?" He watched the play of shadows along her body as moonbeams shone through the slight part in the velvet curtains of the luxury suite.

"Let's revisit some of our anniversary celebrations by taking train rides through the Outback and through Europe." She rested her head on his chest, her blond hair splaying over him in a shimmering spread.

"Except we won't wait until a year has passed." He pressed a kiss to her forehead, breathing in the scent of her shampoo.

She sighed, her breath warm along his skin. "Perfection."

"Like you," he responded, meaning every word.

She grinned up at him. "You're such a romantic."

He hadn't been, not before, but that was another thing he was working on for his wife. Because she deserved it.

She deserved everything, because she was *his* everything.

He reached for a rose from the vase by their bed. "How about I shower you with more of that romance, Mrs. Mikkelson?"

Shana plucked the flower from his hand and traced the bud down his chest. "How about I romance you, Mr. Mikkelson?"

She nudged him to his back, and he took her up on her oh-so-tempting offer, looking forward to paying her back in kind.

Luckily, they had a lifetime for romance ahead of them.

* * * * *

*Passion and turmoil abound in the lives
of the Alaskan Oil Barons!
Nothing is as it seems.
Will they find Milla Jones? Is Uncle Lyle involved?
Is Breanna alive?
Find out the answers and so much more in
the final four stories
starring the Steeles and Mikkelsons!*

The Second Chance

The Rancher's Seduction
(available December 2018)

The Billionaire Renegade
(available January 2019)

The Secret Twin
(available February 2019)

ALASKAN OIL BARONS - STEELE MIKKELSON FAMILY TREE

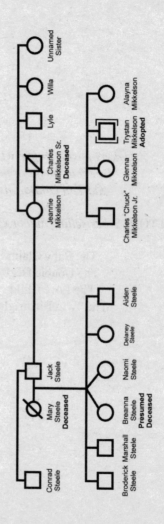

In her brand-new series, New York Times *bestselling author Brenda Jackson welcomes you to Catalina Cove, where even the biggest heartbreaks can be healed...*

Turn the page for a sneak peek at Love in Catalina Cove

CHAPTER ONE

New York City

VASHTI ALCINDOR SHOULD be celebrating. After all, the official letter she'd just read declared her divorce final, which meant her three-year marriage to Scott Zimmons was over. Definitely done with. As far as she was concerned the marriage had lasted two years too long. She wouldn't count that first year since she'd been too in love to dwell on Scott's imperfections. Truth be told there were many that she'd deliberately overlooked. She'd been so determined to have that happily-ever-after that she honestly believed she could put up with anything.

But reality soon crept into the world of make-believe, and she discovered she truly couldn't. Her husband was a compulsive liar who could look you right in the eyes and lie with a straight face. She didn't want to count the number of times she'd caught him in the act. When she couldn't take the deceptions any longer she had packed her things and left. When her aunt Shelby died five months later, Scott felt entitled to half of the inheritance Vashti received in the will.

It was then that Vashti had hired one of the best divorce attorneys in New York, and within six weeks his private investigator had uncovered Scott's scandalous activities. Namely, his past and present affair with his boss's wife. Vashti hadn't wasted any time making Scott aware that she was not only privy to this information, but had photographs and videos to prove it.

Knowing she wouldn't hesitate to expose him as the lowlife that he was, Scott had agreed to an uncontested divorce and walked away with nothing. The letter she'd just read was documented proof that he would do just about anything to hold on to his cushy Wall Street job.

Her cell phone ringing snagged her attention, the ringtone belonging to her childhood friend and present Realtor, Bryce Witherspoon. Vashti clicked on her phone as she sat down at her kitchen table with her evening cup of tea. "Hey, girl, I hope you're calling with good news."

Bryce chuckled. "I am. Someone from the Barnes Group from California was here today and—"

"California?"

"Yes. They're a group of developers that's been trying to acquire land in the cove for years. They made you an unbelievably fantastic offer for Shelby by the Sea."

Vashti let out a loud shout of joy. She couldn't believe she'd been lucky enough to get rid of both her ex-husband and her aunt's property in the same day.

"Don't get excited yet. We might have problems," Bryce said.

Vashti frowned. "What kind of problems?"

"The developers want to tear down your aunt's bed-and-breakfast and—"

"Tear it down?" Vashti felt a soft kick in her stomach. Selling her aunt's bed-and-breakfast was one thing, having it demolished was another. "Why would they want to tear it down?"

"They aren't interested in the building, Vash. They want the eighty-five acres it sits on. Who wouldn't with the Gulf of Mexico in its backyard? I told you it would be a quick sale."

Vashti had known someone would find Shelby by the Sea a lucrative investment but she'd hoped somehow the inn would survive. With repairs it could be good as new. "What do they want to build there instead?"

"A luxury tennis resort."

Vashti nodded. "How much are they offering?" she asked, taking a sip of her tea.

"Ten million."

Vashti nearly choked. "Ten million dollars? That's nearly double what I was asking for."

"Yes, but the developers are eyeing the land next

to it, as well. I think they're hoping that one day Reid Lacroix will cave and sell his property. When he does, the developers will pounce on the opportunity to get their hands on it and build that golf resort they've been trying to put there for years. Getting your land will put their foot in the door so to speak."

Vashti took another sip of her tea. "What other problems are there?"

"This one is big. Mayor Proctor got wind of their offer and figured you might sell. He's calling a meeting."

"A meeting?"

"Yes, of the Catalina Cove zoning board. Although they can't stop you from selling the inn, they plan to block the buyer from bringing a tennis resort in here. The city ordinance calls for the zoning board to approve all new construction. This won't be the first time developers wanted to come into the cove and build something the city planners reject. Remember years ago when that developer wanted to buy land on the east end to build that huge shopping mall? The zoning board stopped it. They're determined that nothing in Catalina Cove changes."

"Well, it should change." As far as Vashti was concerned it was time for Mayor Proctor to get voted out. He had been mayor for over thirty years. When Vashti had left Catalina Cove for college fourteen years ago, developers had been trying to buy up the land for a number of progressive projects. The people of Catalina Cove were the least open-minded group she knew.

Vashti loved living in New York City where things were constantly changing and people embraced those changes. At eighteen she had arrived in the city to attend New York University and remained after getting a job with a major hotel chain. She had worked her way up to her six-figure salary as a hotel executive. At thirty-two she considered it her dream job. That wasn't bad for someone who started out working the concierge desk.

"Unless the Barnes Group can build whatever they want without any restrictions, there won't be a deal for us."

Vashti didn't like the sound of that. Ten million was ten million no matter how you looked at it. "Although I wouldn't want them to tear down Shelby, I think my aunt would understand my decision to do what's best for me." And the way Vashti saw it, ten million dollars was definitely what would be best for her.

"Do you really think she would want you to tear down the inn? She loved that place."

Vashti knew more than anyone how much Shelby by the Sea had meant to her aunt. It had become her life. "Aunt Shelby knew there was no way I would ever move back to Catalina Cove after what happened. Mom and Dad even moved away. There's no connection for me to Catalina Cove."

"Hey, wait a minute, Vash. I'm still here."

Vashti smiled, remembering how her childhood friend had stuck with her through thick and thin. "Yes, you're still there, which makes me think you need your head examined for not moving away when you could have."

"I love Catalina Cove. It's my home and need I remind you that for eighteen years it was yours, too."

"Don't remind me."

"Look, I know why you feel that way, Vash, but are you going to let that one incident make you have ill feelings about the town forever?"

"It was more than an incident, Bryce, and you know it." For Vashti, having a baby out of wedlock at sixteen had been a lot more than an incident. For her it had been a life changer. She had discovered who her real friends were during that time. Even now she would occasionally wonder how different things might have been had her child lived instead of died at birth.

"Sorry, bad choice of words," Bryce said, with regret in her voice.

"No worries. That was sixteen years ago." No need to tell Bryce that on occasion she allowed her mind to wander to that period of her life and often grieved for the child she'd lost. She had wanted children and Scott had promised they would start a family one day. That had been another lie.

"Tell me what I need to do to beat the rezoning board on this, Bryce," Vashti said, her mind made up.

"Unfortunately, to have any substantial input, you

need to meet with the board in person. I think it will be beneficial if the developers make an appearance, as well. According to their representative, they're willing to throw in a few perks that the cove might find advantageous."

"What kind of perks?"

"Free membership to the resort's clubhouse for the first year, as well as free tennis lessons for the kids for a limited time. It will also bring a new employer to town, which means new jobs. Maybe if they were to get support from the townsfolk, the board would be more willing to listen."

"What do you think are our chances?"

"To be honest, even with all that, it's a long shot. Reid Lacroix is on the board and he still detests change. He's still the wealthiest person in town, too, and has a lot of clout."

"Then why waste my and the potential buyer's time?"

"There's a slim chance time won't be wasted. K-Gee is on the zoning board and he always liked you in school. He's one of the few progressive members on the board and the youngest. Maybe he'll help sway the others."

Vashti smiled. Yes, K-Gee had liked her but he'd liked Bryce even more and they both knew it. His real name was Kaegan Chambray. He was part of the Pointe-au-Chien Native American tribe and his family's ties to the cove and surrounding bayou went back generations, before the first American settlers.

Although K-Gee was two years older than Vashti and Bryce, they'd hung together while growing up. When Vashti had returned to town after losing her baby, K-Gee would walk Vashti and Bryce home from school every day. Even though Bryce never said, Vashti suspected something happened between Bryce and K-Gee during the time Vashti was away at that unwed home in Arkansas.

"When did K-Gee move back to Catalina Cove, Bryce?"

"Almost two years ago to help out his mom and to take over his family's seafood supply business when his father died. His mother passed away last year. And before you ask why I didn't tell you, Vash, you know why. You never wanted to hear any news regarding what was happening in Catalina Cove."

No, she hadn't, but anything having to do with K-Gee wasn't just town news. Bryce should have known that. "I'm sorry to hear about his parents. I really am. I'm surprised he's on the zoning board."

For years the townsfolk of the cove had never recognized members of the Pointe-au-Chien Native American tribe who lived on the east side of the bayou. Except for when it was time to pay city taxes. With K-Gee on the zoning board that meant change was possible in Catalina Cove after all.

"I need to know what you want to do, Vash," Bryce said, interrupting her thoughts. "The Barnes Group is giving us twenty days to finalize the deal or they will withdraw their offer."

Vashti stood up to cross the kitchen floor and put her teacup in the kitchen sink. "Okay, I'll think about what you said. Ten million dollars is a lot of money."

"Yes, and just think what you could do with it."

Vashti was thinking and she loved all the possibilities. Although she loved her job, she could stop working and spend the rest of her life traveling to all those places her aunt always wanted to visit but hadn't, because of putting Shelby by the Sea first. Vashti wouldn't make the same mistake.

THE NEXT MORNING, for the first time in two years, Vashti woke up feeling like she was in control of her life and could finally see a light—a bright one at that—at the end of the road. Scott was out of her life, she had a great job, but more importantly, some developer group was interested in her inn.

Her inn.

It seemed odd to think of Shelby by the Sea as hers when it had belonged to her aunt for as long as she could remember. Definitely long before Vashti was born. Her parents' home had been a mile away, and growing up she had spent a lot of her time at Shelby; especially during her teen years when she worked as her aunt's personal assistant. That's when she'd fallen in love with the inn and had thought it was the best place in the world.

Until…

Vashti pushed the "until" from her mind, refusing to go there and hoping Bryce was wrong about her having to return to Catalina Cove to face off with the rezoning board. There had to be another way and she intended to find it. Barely eighteen, she had needed to escape the town that had always been her safe haven because it had become a living hell for her.

An hour later Vashti had showered, dressed and was walking out her door ready to start her day at the Grand Nunes Luxury Hotel in Manhattan. But not before stopping at her favorite café on the corner to grab a blueberry muffin and a cup of coffee. Catalina Cove was considered the blueberry capital in the country, and even she couldn't resist this small indulgence from her hometown. She would be the first to admit that although this blueberry muffin was delicious, it was not as good as the ones Bryce's mother made and sold at their family's restaurant.

With the bag containing her muffin in one hand and her cup of coffee in the other, Vashti caught the elevator up to the hotel's executive floor. She couldn't wait to get to work.

She'd heard that the big man himself, Gideon Nunes, was in town and would be meeting with several top members of the managerial and executive team, which would include her.

It was a half hour before lunch when she received a call to come to Mr. Nunes's office. Ten minutes later she walked out of the CEO's office stunned, in a state of shock. According to Mr. Nunes, his five hotels in the States had been sold, including this one. He'd further stated that the new owner was bringing in his own people, which meant her services were no longer needed.

In other words, she'd been fired.

CHAPTER TWO

A week later

Vashti glanced around the Louis Armstrong New Orleans International Airport. Although she'd never returned to Catalina Cove, she'd flown into this airport many times to attend a hotel conference or convention, or just to get away. Even though Catalina Cove was only an hour's drive away, she'd never been tempted to take the road trip to revisit the parish where she'd been born.

Today, with no job and more time on her hands than she really needed or wanted, in addition to the fact that there was ten million dollars dangling in front of her face, she was returning to Catalina Cove to attend the zoning board meeting and plead her case, although the thought of doing so was a bitter pill to swallow. When she'd left the cove she'd felt she didn't owe the town or its judgmental people anything. Likewise, they didn't owe her a thing. Now fourteen years later she was back and, to her way of thinking, Catalina Cove did owe her something.

COMING NEXT MONTH FROM

HARLEQUIN

Desire

Available December 4, 2018

#2629 HIS UNTIL MIDNIGHT

Texas Cattleman's Club: Bachelor Auction • by Reese Ryan

When shy beauty Tessa Noble gets a makeover and steps in for her brother at a bachelor auction, she doesn't expect her best friend, rancher Ryan Bateman, to outbid *everyone*. But Ryan's attempt to protect her ignites a desire that changes everything...

#2630 THE RIVAL'S HEIR

Billionaires and Babies • by Joss Wood

World-renowned architect Judah Huntley thought his ex's legacy would be permanent trust issues, not a baby! But when rival architect Darby Brogan steps in to help—for the price of career advice—playing house becomes hotter than they imagined...

#2631 THE RANCHER'S SEDUCTION

Alaskan Oil Barons • by Catherine Mann

When former rodeo king Marshall is injured, he reluctantly accepts the help of a live-in housekeeper to prepare his ranch for a Christmas fund-raiser. But soon he's fighting his desire for this off-limits beauty, and wondering what secrets Tally is hiding...

#2632 A CHRISTMAS PROPOSITION

Dallas Billionaires Club • by Jessica Lemmon

Scandal! The mayor's sister is marrying his nemesis! Except it's just a rumor, and now the heiress needs a real husband, fast. Enter her brother's sexy best friend, security expert Emmett Keaton. It's the perfect convenient marriage...until they can't keep their hands to themselves!

#2633 BLAME IT ON CHRISTMAS

Southern Secrets • by Janice Maynard

When Mazie Tarleton was sixteen, J.B. Vaughan broke her heart. Now she has him right where she wants him. But when they're accidentally locked in together, the spark reignites. Will she execute the perfect payback, or will he make a second chance work?

#2634 NASHVILLE REBEL

Sons of Country • by Sheri WhiteFeather

Sophie Cardinale wants a baby. Best friend and country superstar Tommy Talbot offers to, well, *help* her out. But what was supposed to be an emotions-free, fun fling suddenly has a lot more strings attached than either of them expected!

Get 4 FREE REWARDS!

We'll send you 2 FREE Books <u>plus</u> 2 FREE Mystery Gifts.

Harlequin® Desire books feature heroes who have it all: wealth, status, incredible good looks... everything but the right woman.

FREE Value Over **$20**

YES! Please send me 2 FREE Harlequin® Desire novels and my 2 FREE gifts (gifts are worth about $10 retail). After receiving them, if I don't wish to receive any more books, I can return the shipping statement marked "cancel." If I don't cancel, I will receive 6 brand-new novels every month and be billed just $4.55 per book in the U.S. or $5.24 per book in Canada. That's a savings of at least 13% off the cover price! It's quite a bargain! Shipping and handling is just 50¢ per book in the U.S. and 75¢ per book in Canada*. I understand that accepting the 2 free books and gifts places me under no obligation to buy anything. I can always return a shipment and cancel at any time. The free books and gifts are mine to keep no matter what I decide.

225/326 HDN GMYU

Name (please print)

Address   Apt. #

City   State/Province   Zip/Postal Code

> Mail to the **Reader Service:**
> **IN U.S.A.:** P.O. Box 1341, Buffalo, NY 14240-8531
> **IN CANADA:** P.O. Box 603, Fort Erie, Ontario L2A 5X3

Want to try two free books from another series? Call 1-800-873-8635 or visit www.ReaderService.com.

---

*Terms and prices subject to change without notice. Prices do not include applicable taxes. Sales tax applicable in N.Y. Canadian residents will be charged applicable taxes. Offer not valid in Quebec. This offer is limited to one order per household. Books received may not be as shown. Not valid for current subscribers to Harlequin Desire books. All orders subject to approval. Credit or debit balances in a customer's account(s) may be offset by any other outstanding balance owed by or to the customer. Please allow 4 to 6 weeks for delivery. Offer available while quantities last.

Your Privacy—The Reader Service is committed to protecting your privacy. Our Privacy Policy is available online at www.ReaderService.com or upon request from the Reader Service. We make a portion of our mailing list available to reputable third parties that offer products we believe may interest you. If you prefer that we not exchange your name with third parties, or if you wish to clarify or modify your communication preferences, please visit us at www.ReaderService.com/consumerschoice or write to us at Reader Service Preference Service, P.O. Box 9062, Buffalo, NY 14240-9062. Include your complete name and address.

HD18

Scandal! The mayor's sister is marrying his nemesis!
Except it's just a rumor, and now the heiress needs
a real husband, fast. Enter her brother's sexy
best friend, security expert Emmett Keaton. It's the
perfect convenient marriage...until they can't keep
their hands to themselves!

Read on for a sneak peek of
A Christmas Proposition *by Jessica Lemmon,*
part of her Dallas Billionaires Club series!

His eyes dipped briefly to her lips, igniting a sizzle in the air that
had no place being there after he'd shared the sad story of his past.
Even so, her answering reaction was to study his firm mouth in
contemplation. The barely there scruff lining his angled jaw. His
dominating presence made her feel fragile yet safe at the same time.

The urge to comfort him—to comfort herself—lingered. This
time she didn't deny it.

With her free hand she reached up and cupped the thick column
of his neck, tugging him down. He resisted, but only barely, stopping
short a brief distance from her mouth to mutter one word.

"Hey…"

She didn't know if he'd meant to follow it with "this is a bad
idea" or "we shouldn't get carried away," but she didn't wait to find
out.

Her lips touched his gently and his mouth answered by puckering
to return the kiss. Her eyes sank closed and his hand flinched against
her palm.

He tasted…amazing. Like spiced cider and a capable, strong, heartbroken man who kept his hurts hidden from the outside world.

Eyes closed, she gripped the back of his neck tighter, angling her head to get more of his mouth. And when he pulled his hand from hers to come to rest on her shoulder, she swore she might melt from lust from that casual touch. His tongue came out to play, tangling with hers in a sensual, forbidden dance.

She used that free hand to fist his undershirt, tugging it up and brushing against the plane of his firm abs, and Emmett's response was to lift the hem of her sweater, where his rough fingertips touched the exposed skin of her torso.

A tight, needy sound escaped her throat, and his lips abruptly stopped moving against hers.

He pulled back, blinking at her with lust-heavy lids. She touched her mouth and looked away, the heady spell broken.

She'd just kissed her brother's best friend—a man who until today she might have jokingly described as her mortal enemy.

Worse, Emmett had kissed her back.

It was okay for this to be pretend—for their wedding to be an arrangement—but there was nothing black-and-white between them any longer. There was real attraction—as volatile as a live wire and as dangerous as a downed electric pole.

Whatever line they'd drawn by agreeing to marry, she'd stepped way, way over it.

He sobered quickly, recovering faster than she did. When he spoke, he echoed the words in her mind.

"That was a mistake."

Don't miss what happens next!
A Christmas Proposition by Jessica Lemmon,
part of her Dallas Billionaires Club series!

Available December 2018 wherever
Harlequin® Desire books and ebooks are sold.

www.Harlequin.com

  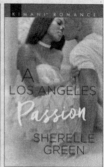
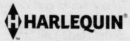

Love Harlequin romance?

DISCOVER.

Be the first to find out about promotions, news and exclusive content!

Facebook.com/HarlequinBooks

Twitter.com/HarlequinBooks

Instagram.com/HarlequinBooks

Pinterest.com/HarlequinBooks

ReaderService.com

EXPLORE.

Sign up for the Harlequin e-newsletter and download a free book from any series at **TryHarlequin.com.**

CONNECT.

Join our Harlequin community to share your thoughts and connect with other romance readers!
Facebook.com/groups/HarlequinConnection

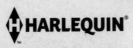

HARLEQUIN®

ROMANCE WHEN YOU NEED IT

HSOCIAL2018

Earn points on your purchase of new Harlequin
books from participating retailers.

Turn your points into **FREE BOOKS**
of your choice!

Join for FREE today at
www.HarlequinMyRewards.com.

Harlequin My Rewards is a free program (no fees)
without any commitments or obligations.